The
MACHIAVELLIAN
MARQUESS

by

Freda Michel

FAWCETT COVENTRY • NEW YORK

THE MACHIAVELLIAN MARQUESS

THIS BOOK CONTAINS THE COMPLETE TEXT OF
THE ORIGINAL HARDCOVER EDITION.

Published by Fawcett Coventry Books, a unit of CBS Publications, the Consumer Publishing Division of CBS Inc., by arrangement with Robert Hale & Company.

ISBN: 0-449-50014-4

Printed in the United States of America

First Fawcett Crest printing: October 1977

First Fawcett Coventry printing: December 1979

10   9   8   7   6   5   4   3   2

CHAPTER ONE

As the doors of the Debtors' Prison at York slammed upon the hunched frail figure of Sir William Wansford, incarcerating him within its comparatively new walls, his daughters, Christina and Rebecca, had but just arrived in Hampshire and were toiling along a seemingly unending driveway towards a huge Baroque mansion—though it was barely discernible upon a distant hill. The night was typical for February, urging them to draw their drab brown capuchins more securely about them in defiance of the icy blast which frolicked with their voluminous petticoats, billowing them out like overgrown pumpkins.

"Do make haste, Rebecca," goaded Christina impatiently, the taller of the two. "We've miles to go yet and it's growing darker every minute!"

"I can't possibly walk any faster, Chris," came the petulant response from her sixteen-year-old sister, struggling with her load of baggage. "You forget, your legs are yards longer than mine, and I've got more to carry."

"Th-That's not true, Becky!" spluttered the other, accustomed to having her commands obeyed—being four years the elder. "You might manage to keep up with me if you saved your breath for walking instead of talking."

Rebecca Wansford braced her small frame against the wintry elements and renewed her efforts to keep abreast of her sister—but she could not remain silent for long.

"At the very least he could have sent a dog-cart and servant to meet us," she complained between pants, "—he being a Marquess, and a rich one too—just look at all this land!"

Christina readily agreed, but refrained from saying so and instead sought to establish a reason for their godfather's oversight.

"Perhaps he thought we'd be in a position to hire a chaise."

Rebecca giggled despite her discomfort. " 'Ens an' 'ogs! What a shock he'll get, won't he, Chris?"

"Hens and *what?*" ejaculated Christina.

"No, not hens, Chris," amended the other obligingly, "—it's 'ens, 'ens an' 'ogs!"

"Where did you acquire such a vulgar expression?"

"Jenny the kitchenmaid. 'Ens an' 'ogs! she cried, when Prickles the cat—"

"If you say it just once more, Becky, I shall wallop you with this bandbox. You are not a kitchenmaid," pointed out her sister in the strongest disapproval. "You are god-child of the Marquess of Stryde, and don't you dare forget it!"

"N-No, Chris," Rebecca mumbled obediently, then fell discreetly quiet as the grand residence of their godparent loomed gradually nearer. "D-Do you think he'll like me?" she probed at length, nurturing sudden doubts.

6

"Of course he will, Becky, if you control yourself, and do not make sheep's eyes at the footmen as you did at Jem Stiggins."

Rebecca thrilled inwardly at the recollection. Having but recently gained a foothold upon the ladder of womanhood she was beginning to realise her potential and the strangely exhilarating effect her liberal endowment of charms produced upon members of the opposite sex, and—despite her sister's adverse warning—intended putting it to the test upon each and every gentleman she was to meet, perhaps, even My Lord Marquess himself?

"H-How do you imagine he'll be, Chris? Do you think *he'll* like *us?*"

Christina swallowed hard, striving to suppress her own qualms on this score, all at once conscious of the Marquess's letter to her father tucked in the pocket of her gown.

"Oh, I don't know!" she replied, testily, trying to hold on to her bulging valise and two bandboxes whilst playing tug-o'-war over her cloak with the wind. "All I know is that he is a marquess who lives at Barrington Hall, which you see before you, is absurdly rich, and—"

"Ooh, Chris!" shrieked Rebecca above the howling gale, her blue eyes gleaming over her flushed dimpled cheeks. "Just think if one of us were to wed him."

Despite the anxiety gnawing within her, a spontaneous laugh escaped Christina.

"What a preposterous notion, Becky. Having been a friend of father some twenty or thirty years ago, and actually having met grandfather before he died, he must be well beyond sixty by now."

"Ugh!" grimaced the other. "How dreadfully dull! One foot in cobwebs and the other bundled up with gout."

7

"Rebecca!" shouted Christina, more in horror than to make herself heard. "For heaven's sake take care what you say! The last thing we must do is offend the old gentleman. He is our only hope now that f-father . . . h-has . . ." her voice trailed pathetically away to end in a sniff.

"I—I promise, Chris," submitted Rebecca contritely, hoping she had not upset her sister yet again, before enquiring cautiously: "Where has father gone, Chris? An-And why was he anxious to see us leave and wanting us to stay, all at the same time—and crying?"

"You have asked that fifty times since we left Whitegables, Becky," protested Christina irritably, at a loss for an answer and battling to master the outsized lump in her throat.

"But you have yet to give me an answer. Is he unwell? Is it the sickness he suffers?"

"Y-Yes!" Christina seized hold of the excuse. "He's been obliged to go away awhile . . . f-for his h-health. . . .

With a superhuman effort she held back the tears. It was imperative she keep the pact made with her father— to divulge nothing of his impending doom to Rebecca, the darling of the family. To her immense relief, her sister appeared satisfied with the explanation, and the conversation again lapsed while the gale raged more fiercely than ever.

"Cheer up, Becky! Not much farther now," Christina encouraged, rallying herself as she strained her eyes in the gathering darkness, trying to form some impression of the house. "Look, we're almost there! Only another hundred yards to go. . . ."

The two gave a final spurt to their steps and eagerly gained the haven of the huge pillared portico which towered over them like some great Roman temple. Setting down her baggage Christina sought to repair the damage to their appearance as best she might in the dim light of the overhanging lantern, hoping to create a favourable impression with his lordship—whose eyesight would no doubt be failing—tucking tendrils of her dark red hair into place whilst casting a critical eye over Rebecca, whose sweet round face, framed by fair frothy curls, wore an expression of pathetic appeal, as she bit her bottom lip to still its trembling.

When tolerably satisfied, Christina squared her tall frame and gave a loud bang at the door with the lion's-head knocker then stepped back to await developments, casting her sister a smile of reassurance—though her own heart pounded like a regimental drumbeat.

"Ch-Chris?" whispered Rebecca, through her chattering teeth, as the clamour died away through the vast interior—which sounded suspiciously empty. "I-I'm frightened . . ."

"There's nothing to be afraid of, Becky," Christina comforted her, hoping she sounded a deal more confident than she felt. "Sh-Sh! I think I hear someone coming!"

A faint tap-tap graduated into a loud martial footstep resounding upon marble, swiftly followed by the clang and rattle of bolts before the ponderous door swung ajar sufficiently to accommodate the powdered head and shoulders of a liveried footman who cast them a haughty glance, noted their bedraggled state, and was about to close the door upon them when Christina spoke up loudly.

"We wish to see the Marquess of Stryde."

At this they were favoured with a more thorough examination—but just as supercilious, goading Christina to indignation.

"Kindly inform your master that the Misses Wansford have arrived from York. He is expecting us."

The flunky returned a blank stare, evidently unimpressed.

"Come along, my man!" she protested, becoming more irate every second. "Must we stand out here all night?"

"You might be obleeged to, ma'am, for I cannot—"

"Now see here!" she burst forth, green eyes flaring. "Our appearance may be a little misleading, but we are not to be trifled with. I demand to see the Marquess, at once!"

"Demand as much as you please," rejoined the servant, rankled at being thus addressed by a storm-tossed waif. "But you cannot see his lordship tonight."

"Can't I?" she cried, losing her temper.

And seizing valise and bandboxes she charged her way through into the house, urging Rebecca to follow suit, utterly impervious to the footman's protests.

The inhabitants would have been deaf indeed not to have heard the commotion in the hall, consequently, a door near at hand opened at this point and out stepped an elegant gentleman in grey brocade, of average height, slender build, and aged about thirty, whose fashionably powdered head turned to each of the group as he disdainfully queried the reason for the disturbance—enamelled snuff-box poised open in his left hand as if about to regale himself therefrom when the commotion occurred.

The lackey, hastening to divulge his version, was promptly silenced by the gentleman, leaving Christina at liberty to state her business.

Eager to oblige, she turned to confront the gentleman

10

and found herself gazing up into a pair of understanding brown eyes set in a face—if not exactly handsome certainly very pleasing, even if tinged with scepticism, as at present.

"I apologise for the noisy intrusion, sir, but we were refused admittance, and we have journeyed far—from York, in fact. I am Miss Christina Wansford—" she presented herself with a curtsy, "—and this is my sister, Rebecca." Rebecca stepped hastily forward to pay her respects and flash her provocative blue eyes at the gentleman. "We wish to be taken to the Marquess, sir, if it please you," completed Christina.

The gentleman looked rather confused, frowning slightly, evidently not pleased at all as he began to detect an educated well-bred female beneath the dust and dishevelment of the road.

"Forgive me, ma'am," he replied, with a hesitant bow. "I—I'm not s-sure . . . if . . . but allow me to introduce myself. I am Anthony Wilde, an intimate friend of his lordship, and completely at your service,"—again he bowed, and again Christina curtsied. "If you would kindly confide your business to me I should be honoured to convey it to Lord Stryde as soon as may be—"

"C-Couldn't I convey it myself? Now?" she interposed quickly, not relishing the idea of the Marquess receiving the news of her advent at second-hand.

"Alas, that is not possible, ma'am. You see—"

"What I've already explained to the lady, Mr. Wilde," broke in the lackey, to meet with a curt dismissal.

Barely had the menial passed out of earshot when Christina embarked upon her explanation.

"But Mr. Wilde, the Marquess is expecting us! He in-

11

vited us here quite explicitly by letter, signed on his own hand—"

Christina broke off, concern for her own well-being suddenly relinquished in favour of that of Mr. Wilde who seemed about to faint, while his hitherto pleasing countenance progressed through several peculiar hues.

"Th-There must be s-some mis-mistake?—m-misunderstanding?" he gasped finally, unable to comprehend the facts for some reason.

Christina eyed him questioningly. "This is Barrington Hall, is it not? County seat of the Marquess of Stryde?"

Unable to voice his acquiescence, Mr. Wilde managed a nod.

"Then there can be no mistake, sir," she resumed, wondering if she had come to a madhouse. "I feel certain the Marquess will understand perfectly when you explain it to him."

This, Mr. Wilde seemed loth to do. Indeed the very suggestion brought perspiration to his forehead and he emitted an inarticulate sound which could be interpreted only as a protest. Rapidly recovering himself, he apologised effusively for his ill-manners, begging the young ladies to be seated before he adjourned in feverish haste to the room he had just quitted, forgetfully leaving the door slightly ajar, sufficient for Christina—if she craned her neck a trifle to the left—to overhear what was said.

At first, the voices were too low and mumbled to distinguish anything, until one—of a much older man—unleashed an oath, followed by further mumbling.

"I realise that, my good fellow," exclaimed the elderly, blustering voice at length, "but they can't stay here, damme! It's downright lunacy!"

"But, sir," remonstrated the younger voice of Mr.

Wilde. "We can't possibly turn them out on a night like this. Satan's rampaging about outside with his entire underworld!"

"And he'll be rampaging about inside when Val gets back—take my word on't!" replied the older voice in no uncertain terms, adding on an inquisitive note: "Letter? What letter?"

Here, Mr. Wilde's voice again dropped to a discreet tone, obviously explaining about the letter, during which Christina held her breath, tensed, and Rebecca smothered one yawn, then another, as she snuggled closer to her on the hard wooden settle, gazing nervously round the palatial hall, blinking at the blinding light from the huge chandeliers which glinted on the Italian marble columns decorated with gold, and the grand staircase, so brilliantly white that she began to wonder if it led all the way up to heaven itself!

"Good gad!" ejaculated the older man of a sudden. "It—It's incredible!"

"I agree, but at the same time feel Miss Wansford's word is to be trusted completely."

"Old Wansford's girls, eh?"

"You know the gentleman, sir?"

"Hum—not really. Exchanged civilities once or twice." He went on tut-tutting to himself. "Here's a pretty coil and no mistake."

"What's to be done?"

Once again Christina was denied the privilege of hearing what was said as the voices dropped to an indistinguishable murmur, and she leaned a little further—to suddenly sit bolt upright, digging Rebecca in the ribs to stop her yawning as she detected the footsteps of Mr. Wilde returning.

13

He gave a slight bow and requested them both to accompany him into the room. So, discarding their cloaks, the two rose to follow Mr. Wilde, shaking the folds out of their unadorned outmoded gowns, worn over modest hoops.

The main drawing-room at Barrington Hall was by far the most lavish the two had ever encountered. Even grander than Mrs Broadlake's, thought Rebecca, her eyes flying open in wonder as she recalled the big house where she had taken tea on several occasions; but even Mrs Broadlake's curtains had not graced the windows like liquid gold, nor her tapestries and furniture yielded such richness. Neither had she boasted as many rare works of art, nor candles. And Rebecca certainly could not remember sinking up to her ankles in the lady's carpet!

Christina, however, having enjoyed a tolerable amount of social life, overcame her admiration somewhat quicker, and her eyes having swept once round the room now alighted upon a portly gentleman of about seventy summers disposed in the gilded armchair by the fire—no doubt the owner of the blustering voice—who sported a Ramillies wig upon his head, and bloated red visage beneath it. Aided by an ebony gold-knobbed stick, he struggled to his feet as the young ladies approached. Mr. Wilde, about to perform the introduction, was forestalled by Christina.

"My Lord Marquess, I am Christina Wansford, and this is my younger sister, Rebecca," she began, curtsying low before the dumbfounded gentleman, Rebecca following suit but with her demure smile clearly directed at Mr. Wilde—and for the second time in the last ten minutes the latter experienced acute embarrassment.

"Er—I-I'm afraid this gentleman is not Lord Stryde,

14

Miss Wansford," he corrected as tactfully as he could. "He is Sir Leonard Shawley, of Shawley Manor—a relative of Lord Stryde.'

"I-I beg your pardon, sir," stammered she, ready to die with mortification, especially as she now noticed the old gentleman was dressed in black with weepers adorning his sleeves, obviously in mourning. "I-I assumed—"

"Haw! Quite understandable, m'dear," commented Sir Leonard, trying to put her at her ease but apparently as nervous as she if the way in which he tweaked continuously at his left ear was aught to go by. "Unfortunately—or p'raps fortunately might be a better word, eh, Wilde?—his lordship is away from home at present, and is not due back for some time."

"I see," she murmured, sinking pensively on to the chair Mr Wilde placed at her disposal, whilst Rebecca made herself comfortable on the tapestried settee by the fire, nurturing a forlorn hope that he might fill the vacant seat beside her.

Following this brief exchange of courtesies the gentlemen joined Christina in a brown study—Mr Wilde frowning before the fire, gnawing at his thumb nail, oblivious to the younger Miss Wansford's concerted efforts to catch his attention, while Sir Leonard limped up and down the extensive room in acute agitation. All, therefore, to be heard was the mechanical ticking of the dainty china and gilt clocks set at intervals about the room, the crackling of the burning logs and the regular, interminable thud, thud, of Sir Leonard's stick as he stumped up and down (serving only to aggravate Mr Wilde's irritation) until he paused suddenly in his tracks, eyeing Christina dubiously.

"You wouldn't—hum—find it convenient to—haw—

15

return home, say, in a day or two?" he probed with caution.

"Home?" mouthed Christina, stupefied. "I-I'm afraid not, sir. M-My father has been—er—called away rather urgently, and the h-house is—is—locked up," she substituted, swiftly.

"Hum, and you have no other relative? No one to whom you could possibly turn other than Lord Stryde?" he pressed, still tweaking mercilessly at his reddened ear.

"No one, indeed," she returned, more puzzled than annoyed. "I trust our arrival does not greatly inconvenience anyone?"

"If I might say so, m'dear, were this my own home, your arrival would give me the utmost pleasure, but alas, as—"

"That's it!" burst our Mr Wilde, suddenly inspired. "You could carry them off to Shawley Manor before Valentine arrives?"

Sir Leonard looked about to throw a fit of apoplexy.

"I say, m'boy, hold y'r infernal horses! What about George?" His voice fell to an undertone, seemingly to spare the young ladies' blushes. "Hum—terrible one for the petticoats, y'know. Probably have to chain him up, b'gad! 'Tis positively indecent the way he chooses to carry on at his age—over forty and still chasing females!" Then, loud enough for all to hear: "High time he took a wife and settled down. Anyways, Wilde, you forget I still have three daughters of me own to find husbands for. Haw! Don't suppose y're interested, what? Time you paraded down the aisle, eh?"

Mr Wilde seemed ready to fade away with humiliation, and muttered something about the present circumstances not being conducive to the discussion of such delicate matters.

"O' course, there's Wylton Weir," pursued Sir Leonard, unoffended.

"The Earl of Wylton's place, you mean?" enthused Mr Wilde, his flame of hope waxing brightly again as he studied this other possibility—until it petered out. "What about Charles?"

Sir Leonard flopped wearily into the nearest chair, relinquishing all hope of a solution.

"Aye, I forgot all about him," he sighed. "Even worse than George, by all accounts. At least George isn't for ever carving somebody up for dinner! According to Edward, everyone he invites to the house runs like the very devil from Charles's deuced swordarm—even the vicar— and he only a step-son! Confounded rake!"

"I'm not surprised!" exclaimed Mr Wilde, delicately pencilled brows shooting aloft. "I shouldn't linger long myself to risk a taste of his deadly steel."

"S'pose not," concurred the other. "Mother let him run amok when his father died. Gad! What a catastrophic state of affairs!"

Christina sat mumchance throughout the duologue, her wide eyes sidling from one gentleman to the other, unable to fully comprehend what was passing between them, and not quite sure if Sir Leonard's final comment applied to her circumstances, his own, or those of the contentious Charles, but thinking the entire exchange rather peculiar and totally irrelevant to the present situation. Howbeit, she not only thought the conversation peculiar but something about the room—and whole house—which had gripped her the moment she had crossed the threshold, but exactly what, she could not say. She cast a glance at

Rebecca, who now seemed to have abandoned hope of ever securing Mr Wilde's attention, and whose eyelids were drooping heavily partly due to sheer physical exhaustion, and partly to the heat of the huge fire beside her.

"I do not see any problem, gentlemen," Christina dared to venture, turning back to take advantage of the interval. "Surely all we need do is await the Marquess who will kindly clarify the situation?"

If she had suggested they all repair to the lake for a moonlight swim the gentlemen could not have looked more horrified.

"That, Miss Wansford," pointed out Mr Wilde with emphasis, "is precisely what we are at great pains to avoid."

"I-I don't understand," she faltered, wishing they would expound their ambiguous statements. "Why shouldn't he be told? Does he suffer ill-health?—and you perhaps think the shock might—"

A strangled laugh erupted from Mr Wilde, and a spluttered cough from Sir Leonard.

"It is your own health which concerns us," Mr Wilde informed her with sincerity.

"My health? Indeed, sir, my health is excellent!"

"But I doubt if it would remain so for very long in the care of Lord Stryde. Do you understand me?"

"I-I'm not sure," she faltered, bewildered. "I-Is he a little strange?"

"Strange? Ha! Not the word I should ha' chosen," interjected Sir Leonard.

Christina swallowed hard before voicing her next thought.

"D-Do you fear for his s-sanity?"

"No, Miss Wansford," stated Mr Wilde gravely. "But he is possessed by a kind of madness at times. His malady—if one could call it that—is not of the brain, but of the soul."

"S-Soul?" gasped she, thankful that Rebecca had fallen off to sleep and was unable to hear these alarming revelations.

"Maybe I should mention that his affliction came via the heart," Mr Wilde added on afterthought.

"Ah, I begin to understand," sighed Christina, sympathetically, picturing in her mind the aged Marquess suffering inconsolably over the loss of someone very dear him—possibly his wife—and suffering herself over her dear father, at once felt a common bond

"Yet I doubt if you fully appreciate the terrible risk you and your sister run in remaining here—if only to your reputations."

"Risk? In what way, sir?"

Mr Wilde shrugged and turned away in despair, leaving the position open to Sir Leonard.

"What Tony here is—hum—trying to say, m'dear," he carried on in a paternal tone, "is that the Marquess does not hold your fair sex in very high—er—esteem. Events beyond our—haw—control have made him the cruel man he is, seeking to lose himself in a life of—er—wickedness. We cannot—hum, haw—overstress the disastrous effect his evil influence could have upon girls of your—hum—tender years."

Mr Wilde, seeking succour in a glass of madeira, suddenly recalled his manners and hurriedly invited Christina to some refreshment, craving forgiveness for the oversight and pleading the unexpected crisis his excuse. Christina thanked him but politely declined, surprised to find food now farthest from her mind when barely an hour ago she had been ravenous enough to devour the very boots on her feet!

"Far from Lord Stryde influencing us with his evil, sir," she suggested naïvely, "—is it not possible that we might well influence him to the good? I begin to suspect him nothing more fearsome than a much misunderstood man in desperate need of loving care and compassion, which my sister and I are willing to give."

The gentlemen stared at her as if now doubting *her* sanity.

"We seem to be at cross purposes, Miss Wansford," gasped Mr Wilde, eventually. "As if we were discussing Satan and the Archangel Gabriel! Your intentions are quite admirable, but alas, I cannot say the same for those of Lord Stryde. I realise you have endured a harrowing journey but do still strongly advise you to digest all we have said, and seriously review your position. Of course, we do not expect you to leave tonight—rooms are already prepared—but I beseech you to make other arrangements as soon as may be."

"And I repeat, sir," declared Christina, a trifle piqued, "we have nowhere else to go."

"Then may I suggest a convent as a reasonable alternative?"

"A convent!" she echoed, aghast. "Having spent a major part of my earlier life in such a place, Mr Wilde, I should need to be threatened by the devil himself before I should consider returning."

"Which will indubitably prove the case, ma'am," he replied promptly, downing another glass of wine to calm his nerves.

"I thank you, gentlemen, for your kind concern," she

resumed, adamantly refusing to be intimidated. "I do not presume to question your word, but nevertheless, find it difficult to credit that my father would have placed us in Lord Stryde's care were his lordship so unfit for the task."

"Indeed, I find it just as difficult to accept," Mr Wilde replied with equal fervour, while Sir Leonard 'hummed and hawed' his support.

But Christina persevered. "Lord Stryde may possibly have been considered wicked in years gone by, but surely now that he is beyond sixty and ageing he has renounced his sinful ways?"

"S-Sixty!" exclaimed Mr Wilde.

"Renounced his what?" ejaculated Sir Leonard.

"I nurture considerable doubt," drawled an alien voice at this stage "—should he live to an hundred and sixty."

This met with a stunned silence before all eyes flew to the doorway which framed the tallest, handsomest—but most infuriatingly arrogant man Christina had ever beheld—and by far the strangest. She could think of only one word to describe him—black! Everything about him from head to foot was black, most unusual of all, the cascades of lace at chin and wrists—everything, except his pale, haughty countenance, little of which was open to view by his shock of long black hair and oversized beaver hat—this cocked with a black favour. He lounged nonchalantly against the doorpost swinging a chased-silver and ebony sword-stick to and fro, while his cruel penetrating eyes revolved slowly to each in turn.

"Well?" he enquired in a voice as arrogant as himself, and with the confident maturity of his thirty-four years. "Would someone deign to explain?"

CHAPTER TWO

Christina, though aware she ought not to stare so shame-lessly, was unable to drag her eyes away from the stranger as his valet hastened to relieve him of cloak, hat and stick. And whilst Sir Leonard and Mr Wilde gaped open-mouthed in disbelief of the painful evidence before them, she remained absorbed in the man himself, wondering how the whole atmosphere was suddenly filled with the aura of his presence—an evil aura—but not entirely un-pleasant.

Sir Leonard was first to retrieve some remnants of voice as he dabbed furiously at his brow with a black-edged handkerchief.

"Y-You arrive at a—hum—inopportune moment, Val-entine. You were not—haw—quite expected."

"Evidently," observed the arrogant gentleman, his gaze lingering significantly on Christina.

"B-But you weren't to return for another week at least—you said so yourself!" protested Mr Wilde, as if the gentleman had committed some crime in not fulfilling the allotted time.

"Faith, that cannot be a note of unwelcome I detect, my dear Tony?"

The gentlemen had the grace to look shamefaced, making no attempt to justify their resentment at the other's intrusion.

"I concluded my business sooner than anticipated," he returned suavely, sauntering into the room, shaking the folds from his full-skirted coat of impeccable black velvet. "And who, may I boldly enquire, is this?" he queried, indicating Christina with a brief nod as he selected a wine to his liking and proceeded to indulge himself, the priceless rings upon his long white fingers flashing in the candlelight.

Mr Wilde nervously cleared his throat. "The young lady is Miss Christina Wansford—"

"Your latest diversion, I presume," he broke in, swaggering across, glass in hand, to appraise her unashamedly from head to toe at closer range. "Hm-m . . . not my type," he mused, his expert eye travelling up and down her length. "But then, none ever was, eh, gentlemen?"

No one, to Christina's further indignation, made any effort to explain the misunderstanding. Instead, Sir Leonard resumed his fidgeting with his ear, while Mr Wilde tugged unmercifully at his white linen stock as if it suddenly choked the life out of him.

"Strange," went on her stern critic, tilting up her dimpled chin with an aristocratic forefinger, "I was under the impression you preferred your women fair, lean and languishing, Tony, not dark, well-developed and—"

"How dare you sir!" blazed Christina, her green eyes

flashing up into his mocking black. "I am not a slave up for auction!"

"—impudent," he concluded, unruffled.

"Neither am I here for anyone's amusement," she went on, "but at the express invitation of Lord Stryde!"

She cherished suspicions that her father had previously written to the Marquess acquainting him with his dire circumstances, thus prompting the invitation, and chose to preserve the impression that the invitation had been a spontaneous act on the part of his lordship—trusting that her father's original letter would remain in confidence between herself and the Marquess.

Sir Leonard, deeming it time he intervened, was arrested in his tracks by a gesture from the newcomer who, to Christina's satisfaction, seemed quite impressed by her last announcement.

"May I enquire how you came by this invitation?" he queried with scepticism.

"My father, Sir William Wansford, received it by letter from his lordship, personally. I have it here . . . s-some . . . where. . . ." She fumbled awhile in the pocket of her patched-up blue homespun before producing the letter and delivering it into his charge—assuming he was not sufficiently astute to perceive beyond the adversity referred to, into the cells of the Debtors' Prison. "My father replied recently, advising the Marquess of our expected arrival."

She had not finished informing him of this when a lackey materialised at the gentleman's side with her father's letter—unopened, which the gentleman, having finished perusing the Marquess's letter, calmly proceeded to open—to her amazement.

"I protest, sir!" she remonstrated angrily. "You have

no right to open my father's letter! You can see quite clearly, it is directed in person to the Marquess of Stryde!"

"In which case," acknowledged the gentleman, blandly, "none other has greater right."

Christina felt her blood slowly draining away.

"I-I don't un-understand," she stammered, wondering how many more times she would need to reiterate this phrase before the night was out.

Anxious to avoid any further embarrassment, Sir Leonard hobbled hastily forward.

"Please forgive my lack of foresight and manners, m'dear," he apologised to Christina. "This, I ought to have mentioned, is my nephew, the Marquess of Stryde."

Christina's legs gave way and she descended to the floor in, what she hoped would be acknowledged, a curtsy—her heart descending in unison.

"I-It's impossible . . ." she mouthed, incredulously.

"How, pray?" he parried, with the travesty of a bow. "Because I do not happen to be senile and absolved of sin?"

"Y-You are my g-godfather?"

"I fear not," he replied in a voice devoid of emotion. "That would be the privilege of my father, the fourth Marquess, who unfortunately expired two months agone."

"Oh, how dreadful!" cried Christina, now appreciating why the strange atmosphere pervaded the house, and her former conversation with Mr Wilde and Sir Leonard had been difficult to comprehend. "M-My father knows n-nothing of this . . . h-he will be m-much st-stricken. . . ."

Likewise his daughter, who looked about to collapse, inducing the Marquess to comment:

"Do not stand on my account, Miss Wansford. Please

be seated." A mere glance, and a footman emerged with a glass of wine which the Marquess placed in her trembling hands before continuing. "My father evidently issued the invitation prior to his demise. I am surprised that your father stands in ignorance of the event for I was given to understand by my steward that all persons of consequence had been notified."

There was no derogatory implication evident in his tone, yet Christina coloured, aware that her father's ignorance was due—not only to living in the wilds of Yorkshire, but to the stringent economy which had governed their lives, forbidding even the purchase of newspapers.

"P-Permit me to of-offer my d-deepest condol . . . ences," she faltered.

The Marquess bowed his acknowledgement.

"There is no need to commiserate," he returned, almost flippantly. "We did not exchange greetings above three times in the last decade. Indeed, it would not surprise me to learn that your father was wholly unaware of mine existence. Alas! I was an entity my sire did not care to boast about; and at the time of their association, I was being initiated in the ways of the world at Eton, Oxford, and the Grand Tour—in that order."

With that, the Marquess devoted his attention to the second letter, whilst the servants entered bearing a substantial supper, creeping soundlessly about their business as if sensing something vital toward.

Having read the letters through, Lord Stryde deliberated awhile before refolding them and pocketing them out of sight. Then, draining his glass, he turned to confront his uncle and Mr Wilde.

"Well, gentlemen, you have dined, I presume?"

"D-Dined?" stuttered Mr Wilde, uncertain if he were hearing aright.

"Eaten, my friend," he clarified, languidly. "That monotonous ritual we must needs endure to survive."

"Oh—er—dined?—Y-Yes. Your uncle and I dined earlier at the customary hour."

"And Miss Wansford?"

"Thank you, my lord, but I have no appetite," she replied, anxiously awaiting judgement on her future like a criminal in the witness-box.

Without more ado he took up position at table amidst a flurry of footmen and was about to commence when his eye lighted upon the inert pink bundle on the settee.

"That, I gather, is the younger Miss Wansford," he remarked casually. "She must retire immediately. I am not accustomed to recumbent bodies littering the drawing-room—except mine own."

Silence prevailed as Rebecca was borne away by the maids to one of the prepared boudoirs.

"You will remain, Miss Wansford," he informed Christina, who was making to follow. "I require some imformation."

"What do you—hum—plan doing with 'em, Val?" Sir Leonard dared ask, voicing the question for everyone.

"I shall decide in due course, uncle," replied his nephew evasively, critically viewing the wide variety of dishes arrayed before him.

"Y-You don't mean to consider keeping them here?" burst out Mr Wilde, strongly.

Lord Stryde smiled disarmingly at his friend, a smile which temporarily banished the cruelty round his mouth.

"Of course not, my dear Tony. Perish the thought."

Mr Wilde and Sir Leonard heaved unanimous sighs of

relief—proved somewhat premature by their host who added:

"They will remain, quite naturally, of their own volition."

It was now Christina's turn to look relieved—which did not escape the notice of the Marquess.

"The prospect evidently appeals to you, Miss Wansford," he observed with languid interest. "May I ask why?"

"Simply because I can't bear to think what the gruesome alternative would have been, my lord."

"And what gives you leave to think that life here will be less so?"

"Exactly what your uncle and I have emphasized all evening—to no purpose," interjected Mr Wilde.

"With the customary colourful account of my life, no doubt, omitting not a single sordid detail," opined the Marquess dryly.

"We deemed it nothing more than our duty as gentlemen to present the young lady with the true facts, Valentine," his friend defended himself, with Sir Leonard's approval. "To enable her to make up her own mind."

"And thus enlightened, she yet decides to stay," mused my lord, curiously eyeing Christina. "Why, I wonder?"

"Because I have no choice," she stated yet again.

"No other reason?" he calmly challenged. "Mayhap, of a more profitable nature?"

"Valentine!" vituperated his friend. "What the devil are you insinuating?"

Christina flamed with resentment. "None whatsoever, my lord!" she rejoined with asperity. "Were it not for the fact that I have my sister's welfare to consider in regard to the inclement conditions outside, I should leave this instant!"

"You must agree, Miss Wansford, that 'tis to our mutual advantage if we understand one another from the outset. I merely seek to determine the type of female I accept into my house."

"And having already determined the type of man you are, Lord Stryde," she retaliated angrily, before she could stop herself, "you cannot in all seriousness believe I should remain here to be so insulted had I any possible alternative!"

A deathly hush greeted this declamation, Sir Leonard and Mr Wilde positively stunned, as no one—let alone a female—had ever dared to shout at Valentine Barrington before. It would appear that life at Barrington Hall was going to be quite interesting in future—if they ever reached an understanding.

Meanwhile, the Marquess remained unperturbed, though his inward surprise did not fall far short of that of his companions.

"F-Forgive me, my lord," begged Christina, now devoured with contrition lest she further prejudice her already extremely precarious position. "W-We wish to inconvenience you no more than is absolutely necessary—"

"I am relieved to hear it."

"—so if you will but bear with us awhile, we should be deeply indebted to you. In return, Becky and I could sing and play upon the spinet to entertain you. We are quite accomplished!"

The Marquess hesitated, eyeing her suspiciously, his glass suspended in mid-air, unable to decide if he were being complimented or insulted by the offer.

"I doubt prodigiously if your range of accomplishments

would embrace my variety of female entertainment," he observed with cynicism.

"I would stress, my lord, that our stay is temporary. We shall be gone as soon as our father returns, or we find suitable husbands."

"I am not prepared to wait that long, I'm afraid, and run the risk of being tormented to an early grave by two wry-faced crotchety old maids. As your guardian—"

"Guardian?"

"Indeed, Miss Wansford. You do not seriously believe that you father had you come all this way purely for a social call?"

"B-But it is a visit! He said so! Until he returns in a matter of months—even weeks . . . h-he promised, on oath!"

"A promise, I am confident, he has every intention of keeping, but until he does—whether you like it or not—your future is in my hands, and I shall plan accordingly."

This prompted Christina to question precisely how much the Marquess had discerned about her family troubles and if his evasion of any reference to the Debtors' Prison was due to ignorance on his part—or a shrewd manoeuvre.

"I repeat, as your guardian, I shall supply the husbands—"

"With all respect, my lord," she interjected on impulse, "I shall prefer to choose my own."

"I've no doubt you would," he accorded indifferently. "However, what you prefer is of little consequence."

"It is of vital consequence!" she exclaimed taking profound exception and unwisely giving licence to her wayward tongue. "My father never would have coerced us into a distasteful marriage! He never would have done such a horrid thing—and would object in the strongest terms if he—"

Sir Leonard and Mr Wilde were not to be disappointed. The explosion they had anticipated all evening now came.

"Silence!" thundered the Marquess, rising abruptly and slamming the table—his black eyes glinting menacingly. "I do not happen to be your father—who is in no position to raise objections! As long as you are under my roof you will obey my orders without question! Is that understood?"

Trembling in awe as his black sinister figure loomed over her like the Prince of Darkness himself, Christina somehow managed to nod. True, she had never met anyone like him; neither had she been shouted at before in her entire life—which seemed to be the only thing she and he had in common.

"One!—you will venture nowhere in the vicinity of my private apartments in any circumstances. Two!—your conduct will be beyond reproach at all times. Three!— should you choose to ride, you will not surpass the boundary of the estate. You may select any horse you fancy from my stables except the black stallion in the end stall—take him at your peril. Four!—you will keep the door of your boudoir locked at all hours of the night, for obvious reasons. Five!—as this is a house of death you will observe the necessary period of mourning ordained by propriety. You will be furnished with all that is needed in this respect. And six!—you will not accept any invitations or try to contact anyone outside the estate without first obtaining my permission. This may be done through my valet, Peter Fraser. You will think me a severe taskmaster, but this you must accept if you remain. Unfortunately, the choice is limited—my house, or the poorhouse."

With that, he sat down to resume the meal, the topic now banished from his mind, and silence once again pervaded the room—but until Christina had done choking on his words and recovered her power of speech. Though she was loth to confess it she had been rather indulged by her father who had granted her more than customary licence since the passing of his wife, when Christina had assumed the burden of running the household. Thus, she had been empowered with the authority to check the impulsive high spirits of her sister, but alas, had no one to check her own—until now. Her submissiveness was, therefore, somewhat short-lived.

"Are we not to attend any balls?—assemblies?—or even visit in the neighbourhood?" she cried indignantly.

"No!" was the firm rejoinder.

" 'Pon rep, Val!" exclaimed his uncle, unable to keep quiet any longer. "Coming it rather strong, what? Can't keep 'em caged up in y'r own harem, m'boy—not done in this country! Hum—not the thing, egad! Tony here tried to tell 'em they'd be better off in a deuced convent but they wouldn't listen—eh, Wilde?"

Further emboldened by Sir Leonard's support, Christina took three paces forward to confront the Marquess over a dish of sugared almonds.

"I refuse to be bound by such primitive conditions!"

"Then kindly collect your paraphernalia from the hall—which I tripped over on my way in," the Marquess coolly apprised her, his attention focused upon a peach he was paring with expert precision, "and find your way out."

"You are unreasonable!" she protested, exasperated, her green eyes flaring anew and the copper lights glinting in her long hair which, being already dishevelled, was now dislodged from its pins and draped her shoulders alluringly, framing her attractive—though wilful—features. "How, then, do you intend finding us husbands?"

"With tempting dowries apiece it should be no difficult matter—" he paused, throwing her a scornful glance—"unless you deem yourself sufficient attraction without it?" he sneered, his eyes meandering over her shapely contours.

"I do not need your dowry, sir, tempting or no!" she rejoined proudly, the colour flooding her cheeks.

"You have an exceedingly high opinion of yourself, young lady."

"Then we should deal famously together, my Lord Marquess!"

The audience gasped—and again Christina apologised for her unruly tongue.

"I begin to understand, Miss Wansford, how it comes about that you are yet unwed," he remarked with a cryptic smile.

"I've had offers, my lord."

"Which you evidently refused—why?"

"B-Because I . . . I . . ."

"Well?"

"I—I wasn't in love."

"And your father accepted this puerile excuse?" he queried with incredulity. "Rest assured, on the next occasion nothing short of a nun's habit will save you from the gaping jaws of a marriage-bed."

"Which would be highly preferable!" she flashed, her spirit of female independence again asserting itself.

The santanic look intensified in his inscrutable eyes.

"I know how to deal with shrews, Miss Wansford," he snarled. "I have broken many spirited fillies in my time, and you will be no exception! The task of finding you a husband will be impossible enough without being thwarted by you at every turn—for who but a fool would take an impoverished draggle-tailed termagant to wife? And should you cherish any intention of spurning my choice of husband you will alternatively find yourself swelling the ranks of my servants!"

Christina had never felt so humiliated—and what was worse, could think of no apt response. Instead, she stood clenching and unclenching her fingers as tears of self-pity stung her eyes—goaded further that he was able to witness her distress.

"I do not intend keeping you in luxury, madam," he rasped harshly. "From henceforth you will be living on my charity, and not for one moment will I allow you to forget it! Unless—" his eyes made his meaning abundantly clear—"you chance to find favour with me. . . ."

"I'd rather die!" she flung back, battling in vain for self-control.

"Which would avail your dependents little," he countered with a sneer.

"M-My father shall h-hear of this," faltered she, on a sob. "He-He will d-demand . . . an . . . ap-apology!"

Sir Leonard hovered nervously in the background, anxiously biting his lip, while Mr Wilde—realising that his intervention would only aggravate the explosive situation—turned away, unable to endure any more.

But the Marquess remained inexorable as he hissed contemptuously: "Inmates languishing in the Debtor's Prison are in no condition to demand anything!"

And with an inarticulate cry, Christina fled from the room.

CHAPTER THREE

Next morning, Christina was rudely awakened by a vigorous shaking from Rebecca to the accompaniment of shouted demands in her ear for her to wake up at once and tell her all that had transpired the night before. But as can be appreciated, Christina was not in a talkative mood and was already decided upon leaving the intimate details of her painful confrontation with the Marquess until the wound to her pride had been given a chance to heal. Not surprisingly, Rebecca did not take very kindly to this and made her objection in the only way she knew—by throwing a violent tantrum—until she spied her sister's inflamed swollen eyes and extremely damp pillow and so, tried to summon an element of discretion, believing the absence of their father to be largely the contributing factor, in which she was not entirely misled.

With a stifled groan Christina managed to manoeuvre herself into a sitting position to sip the hot chocolate already at her bedside. Her head throbbing following one of the worst nights she had ever experienced and her vanity in shreds after the excruciating indignity she had suffered, she paid little heed to Rebecca's excited chatter about the colour and content of her bedchamber, and personal life history of her new maid, Daisy Bigsley. As she slowly sipped the chocolate Christina relived in her mind the harrowing scene of the night before, thus fanning the flames of her already intense hatred for the Marquess. She found words too inadequate to describe the most callous uncivilised being she had ever met, and by the time she had drained the cup was determined more than ever that every ounce of strength and ingenuity she possessed would be used to scheme a way to extricate herself and Rebecca from his tyrannical clutches, and atone for the terrible insults she had borne.

After they had broken their fast, Rebecca eagerly prevailed upon Christina to go riding to which the latter agreed, being just as eager to quit the house and its depressing memories. So they betook themselves to the stables to view their guardian's excellent stock of thoroughbred horseflesh. Christina dubiously regarded the ferocious-looking black stallion housed in the far stall and passionately wished she had courage enough to defy the Marquess and pour balm on her pride by taking it, but common sense over-ruled and she chose a docile roan mare, more suited to her style. By this time, however, Rebecca's heart was already firmly set upon a rather skittish dapple-gray which no amount of persuasion would discourage her from riding. Not wishing to inflict further disappointment on her sister, Christina let her have her way and at length the two cantered off, politely declining the zealous offers of the stablehands to bear them company.

Once under way, they broke into a fast gallop which helped to dispel much of Christina's morbid apprehension about the future. It was a glorious day, especially so for February and in comparison with the previous night. The bright but rather weak sun caressed the verdant pastureland as if it were already spring, coaxing the cheery birds from their nests in search of tasty morsels, uplifting her heart enough to view the happenings following her arrival as nothing but the remains of some grisly nightmare.

Before long, in fact, she had managed to relegate her weird guardian to the back of her mind and was actually about to indulge in a smile, when to her dismay Rebecca's frisky grey suddenly bolted for no apparent reason as they neared the boundary of the estate, carrying her off in a frenzied gallop with her hysterical screams trailing in her wake.

In a flash Christina was after her, goading her mare on furiously whilst castigating herself for not devoting her fullest attention to the animal, half expecting it to take fright at the first obstacle. It was no time at all before Rebecca and the grey were over the hedge bordering the estate and out of sight in the woodland beyond.

"Becky! Becky!" Christina shouted herself hoarse once she was into the woods, pressing on in the direction Rebecca was last seen, but not a sound of horse nor rider was now to be heard. On and on she kept with her feverish search, growing more anxious with every passing second, when a girlish giggle—unmistakably Becky's—fell like balm upon her ear. But when she at last spied her errant sister, she could not quite decide if she were more relieved to find her unharmed, or horrified at her being clasped in the arms of an utter stranger!

"Rebecca!" she cried, aghast. "What on earth—"

"Don't be angry, Chris," exclaimed Becky, springing guiltily away from the gentleman and running to reassure her sister that all was indeed well. "Mr Liddell here, came gallantly to my rescue. And of all the surprising things, he's the Marquess's cousin! Would you believe it? His father is the Earl of Wylton! So you see, it is all quite proper, isn't it?"

Christina supposed it was but still nurtured doubts about the gentleman's intentions, and why he had deemed it necessary to squeeze her sister quite so tightly when merely assisting her to dismount.

"Just imagine, Chris!" babbled on Rebecca, flushed with the excitement of her hair-raising gallop and rescue. "He appeared from nowhere of a sudden and reined the grey to a halt as simple as you please. Rode like the wind, to save my life!" she rhapsodised, appending somewhat sheepishly: "He-He was—er—just helping me down when you arrived."

"I see," acknowledged her sister, flashing a suspicious look at the fashionable beau who seemed more concerned about the mud befouling his glossy black boots than saving anyone's neck, as he dabbed with tender solicitude at the offending stains, using for this delicate operation the largest dandelion leaf to hand.

" 'Ens—er—I mean, strap me vitals, if I've ever been so scared!"

"Rebecca!" reproved Christina again. "Watch your tongue."

"You said I could use fashionable exclamations—"

"Which are refined and ladylike! What will Mr Liddell think of us?"

But there was no qualm to be suffered on that point as the gentleman—garbed in black, in derference to his late uncle—now saw fit to approach, still laughing as he bowed low to Christina and formally introduced- himself.

"Charles Liddell, very much a y'r service, ma'am," he announced in a voice perhaps a trifle high in pitch for one of his goodly size, but which Christina presumed cultivated in favour of the current trend amongst the young fops—though the gentleman himself could scarce expect to see thirty-five again, "—but ye may call me Charles, an it please ye." He paused, waiting to see how she would respond to this familiarity, viewing her with the experienced eye of a man accustomed to getting what he wanted, regardless of cost; then went on: " 'Pon honour! First the sweet buddin' rose, then the incomparable rose in full bloomin' splendour! Rot me, ne'er have I encountered so much captivatin' beauty in but a single moment! I vow it fair snatches me breath away."

"I hope you will survive without it, Mr Liddell," Christina returned his banter. "Are you, perhaps, the gentleman who carves vicars up for dinner?"

At this, he appeared indeed bereft of breath. "By Saint George!" he crowed at length, devouring her dainty fingertips. "Beauty possessed of a lively wit—a rare combination, ma'am. Suffer me to assist ye from y'r worthy steed—"

"Thank you, kind sir, but I do not plan to tarry long," she swiftly discouraged him as he prepared to seize her by the waist. "I am Miss Wansford—Miss Christina Wansford, and I hope you won't think ill of me if I merely express my gratitude for saving my sister, then depart?"

She was beginning to feel extremely uneasy at disobeying the Marquess—to say nothing of the fact that Charles Liddell filled her with some misgiving following the alarming insight into his character she had been accorded by Sir Leonard and Mr. Wilde barely fifteen hours ago. To be thus alone with him in the deserted woods with only Rebecca for protection seemed to be excellent cause for concern.

"You are under the guardianship of my noble cousin, so y'r enchantin' sister tells me," he probed curiously in an attempt to detain her, his contempt unmistakable, which made Christina hesitate and turn to regard him but to her surprise he seemed to have difficulty in meeting her eye and glanced away in pretence of admiring the scenery.

"That is so, sir," she responded, civilly.

"You have met him, I s'pose?"

"Yes; I-I've had the honour," she felt courtesy-bound to state, even if it was an honour she could well have done without.

"Honour!" he echoed, obviously of the same opinion. "I deduce from y'r remark, Miss Wansford, that ye don't know m'cousin very intimately?"

"As I have not yet dwelt twenty-four hours under his roof, Mr Liddell, perhaps that is not surprising," she replied, piqued. "Furthermore, sir, I do not think it proper to discuss my guardian with one who is himself, little more than a stranger."

"Stranger! Gad!" he cried, reverting to his theatricals.

" 'Pon rep, m'dear, didn't quite see m'self as such. A thousand pardons but, damme, I feel I've known ye all me life!" He hastily swept the ground with his purple-laced three-cornered hat and replaced it on his dark brown hair, which was dressed in a fashionable queue. All this subservience impressed Christina and restored a modicum of her confidence in the gentleman—only to have it crumble again when he resumed. "I vow, 'tis common knowledge what the world thinks o' Cousin Valentine. Ye

40

need not fear to declare openly what is in y'r heart, for my infamous cousin's dark mysterious past is regular village gossip."

At that moment Christina had no greater wish than to unburden her heart to someone, but stopped short at Charles Liddell, aware that he could be secretly in league with his cousin, and as his pawn, merely seeking a means to gain her confidence. Consequently, to her annoyance, she impetuously leapt to the absurd extreme of actually defending the Marquess.

"I fail to see how Lord Stryde's infamy is any darker or more mysterious than most other wild bloods of his class—and as I have already heard it rumoured, sir, not excluding your own?"

The gentleman's swift intake of breath almost choked him.

"Burn m'soul, ma'am!" he ejaculated in offended tone, administering laced scented handkerchief to sensuous lips. "We don't all callously contrive to despatch our fathers to the after-life!"

"I-I beg your p-pardon?" gasped Christina, horrified, bethinking Mr Liddell's prejudice against her guardian (whether genuine or not) to be outweighing his reason, as Rebecca drew nearer, eyes and ears agog, her flagging interest suddenly revived.

" 'Pon oath, m'dear!—realise I'm not exactly a saint m'self, and readily own to choppin' short one or two breaths—in defence o' me honour, ye understand—er—quite legitimately. Never, I do solemnly swear, would I stoop to murder in cold blood!—and me own sire, to boot!"

"Th-That's a monstrous accusation to make against Lord Stryde, your own cousin, sir!" cried she enraged, un-

41

able to see any difference betwixt the two methods of extermination. "I refuse to hear any more! Come, Rebecca!"

But he seized the bridle of her horse, determined that she should, his eyes suddenly consumed with such intense hatred that she was loth to gainsay him.

" 'Tis no more than the truth, fair maid," he growled in undertones. "Being the shrewd knave he is, Cousin Valentine saw to't that there was nought to incriminate him— no witnesses, nothing! And so, death by heart failure was recorded."

"But surely that is reasonable to suppose?" breathed Christina, clutching frantically at this straw of hope to banish all thought of the same terrible fate looming on her horizon.

Mr Liddell indulged in a twisted smile. "Is't not strange, ma'am, how my uncle happens to die—hours after threatening to disinherit his son—from a supposed heart attack?"

Christina was speechless with horror. There was some mistake? Some plausible explanation? That Lord Stryde was a little wicked she already comprehended, but never had she imagined the diabolical extent of his wickedness. A peculiar instinct warned her that the word of Charles Liddell was not to be wholly relied upon—but did she err in her judgement? What of Sir Leonard and Mr Wilde? Had not they also stressed the danger she was courting in remaining at Barrington Hall? Going so far as to declare their anxiety for her very life? At the time, she had thought them to be simply exaggerating in their eagerness to get her gone, but now began to appreciate the significance of their warnings and their reluctance to put into words their true feelings in loyalty to the Marquess.

"Confess it, m'dear," he urged her, becoming passionately roused at the recollection, which appeared to affect him deeply. "He had overwhelming motive—atop of which, he flatly refused to deny it, and still does! Hasn't confessed to anything, mark you—but all the same, doesn't protest his innocence!"

The gentleman was extremely convincing, but Christina felt uneasy at the way he seemed unable to look her directly in the eye—yet when she turned away, could feel his gaze upon her, scrutinising her, as if striving to assess the resoluteness of the female he was dealing with.

His passion waned as swiftly as it had risen, and he was now consumed with remorse at having alarmed her, and a warmth pervaded his manner as she sat her horse, apprehensively biting her lip whilst ruminating the facts and how they affected her already perilous plight.

"I vow I have no wish to cause you anxiety, Miss Wansford, but I must speak out in fairness to yourself and your sister, for I know of no other able, or willing, to put you on your guard and make you fully aware of my cousin's treachery. You are a lady of acute perception, ma'am, and having made the acquaintance of my Uncle Leonard—who ne'er has a generous word to offer in my favour—I trust you will not allow his puritanical opinions to influence your judgement against me. Most wild bloods cherish an inborn ember of decency which bursts aflame when one is tempted beyond the limits decreed by convention, saving one's soul from perdition. If you would allow me to presume further 'pon our brief meeting, and beg—nay, beseech you—to call upon me if at any time you find yourself in need of a friend, or assistance, even in the smallest way. You will find me at Wylton Weir, just over yonder hill."

43

This fervent offer made Christina acutely ashamed of her previous lack of faith in the gentleman and she now sought to rectify the misunderstanding, sensing that the day might not be very far distant when she would need to avail herself of his help.

"Thank you most profoundly for your generous offer, Mr Liddell," she replied with fervour, offering her hand. "You are very kind, and I do stand in great need of a friend. I hope we shall meet again."

"Indeed we shall, m'dear," he returned eagerly, bowing over her hand again, "if ye happen to ride this way often, for I exercise my horses on this stretch every day."

Christina looked downcast. "I-I'm afraid it will not be possible, sir. Your cousin has forbidden Becky and me to ride beyond the boundaries of his estate, so you see—"

"Repine not, fair lady! I shall brave dear Valentine's wrath and ride with ye—with y'r kind permission?—on his land. He has threatened to shoot me on sight if I ever dared, but what more could I ask than to gasp m' last cradled in the bosom o' such beauty as thine?"

Christina gave a spontaneous laugh, for Charles Liddell seemed to be the last person in the world to discard life so lightly—and the twinkle in his eye would appear to confirm this.

Here, Rebecca decided it time she made herself heard.

"Mr. Liddell," she piped up, prompting both him and her sister to turn and view her in surprise, having obviously forgotten her presence. "Why should Lord Stryde hate you so?"

Charles Liddell was somewhat confused by the unexpected enquiry.

"Perhaps, child, because I elect to speak the truth which embarrasses him. He is anxious lest I delve too

44

deeply into his affairs, and he is made to hang for his crime."

"But by shooting you, wouldn't he be hanged just the same? And if he did have anything to hide, surely the law would have discovered it by now?" pursued Rebecca, undaunted by her sister's censorious look.

Contrary to the Marquess, it was his cousin who suffered some disconcertion here—colouring slightly, and clearing his throat as if at a loss for something to say.

"Really, Becky!" Christina felled the breach, almost as uneasy as Mr Liddell and wishing to preserve amiable relations. "It is none of your business!"

"Alas, Miss Wansford, you assume aright," he replied to Becky hesitantly, conscious that an answer was called for. "If ye doubt my word, may I suggest ye seek out a certain stablehand by the name o' Milton—Bob Milton? I understand he was at my uncle's deathbed. Alternatively," he added facetiously, gallantly assisting Rebecca onto her horse before mounting his own, "why not obtain y'r information first hand from the perpetrator himself?" And bidding them a pleasant *au revoir* he doffed his hat and cantered off across the woodland glade to disappear amidst the trees.

For some time, Christina's anxious gaze remained fixed in the direction of his broad retreating figure as she nurtured the feeling that she would have need of the assistance of Charles Liddell before she was much older. Then Rebecca broke in on her reverie.

"Do you believe his story, Chris? Do you think the Marquess w-would m-murder anyone?"

Indeed she did; but she would not dream of telling Becky so, realising that nothing was to be gained by unduly alarming her sister with a detailed description of

Lord Stryde, whom she would meet quite soon enough and form her own judgement. Moreover, she had enough worries troubling her at the moment without the addition of an hysterical child on her hands. Instead, she tried to reassure Rebecca by telling her that their father would not have placed them in Lord Stryde's charge had he believed him remotely capable of such a dire crime and not a man of the highest integrity—discreetly making no mention of the fact that their father had probably been in ignorance of the present Marquess's existence—rounding off the matter by making her sister swear on her heart not to divulge a word to anyone of all she had heard, and to try her utmost to forget that she had ever even heard it. This, Rebecca did solemnly swear, and the two returned to Barrrington Hall.

However, this new and most terrifying knowledge about their guardian would have panicked Christina into packing their belongings immediately upon their return and seeking sanctuary at the nearest convent as suggested by Mr Wilde but for the fact that such hasty action would not have improved the lot of their father. Throughout the return ride she could not summon interest in Rebecca's chatter—a colourful account of her fairytale rescue by Charles Liddell (though cherishing a secret wish that her knight-errant had been a certain gentleman with brown eyes)—but remained deep in thought, their dangerous situation painfully apparent.

So, this was the reason behind the promise my lord had wrung from her not to venture beyond the boundaries of the estate, nor make contact with anyone—no doubt to avoid any awkward questions which would arise should they happen to suddenly disappear! Also, why he had brushed aside the topic of husbands as a triviality—because he had a more certain way to dispose of them which would not overstrain his power of ingenuity—nor his wealth. Aware that she had already broken two of his rules, she was now adamantly resolved about one which would *never* be broken—to keep her room door firmly locked.

It could be appreciated that the following morning found the younger Miss Wansford averse to riding after her unnerving experience, and as this suited the elder Miss Wansford's arrangements admirably she did not persist with the invitation but seized the opportunity to ferret out Bob Milton. However, it was not until the second day that she managed to acquire Bob as escort upon her morning ride, to find that it necessitated some two hours meaningless conversation with the man before his diffidence in her presence was overcome. And even then, when she finally broached the delicate subject of his employer, to her chagrin, the timid little man immediately retired into his humble shell again. It was only by bullying him a trifle and threatening to take the matter up with Lord Stryde in person (which she certainly had no intention of doing) that she succeeded in loosening the menial's tongue; but she found him still extremely cautious, disclosing nothing she did not already know. Nevertheless, although Bob Milton was infinitely careful not to say anything which would incriminate his master, yet did his very manner confirm Christina's suspicions and pronounce the Marquess guilty as assuredly as if Bob had named him murderer outright and presented her with undeniable proof! As in the case of Mr Liddell, she was convinced Bob knew much more than he was prepared to say, having undoubtedly been coerced into silence by Lord Stryde. This was perfectly understandable, Bob having a newly-acquired mouth to feed, making a total of nine Milton mouths in all, and consequently his job to safeguard the harder.

During the ensuing days Christina was dull company indeed for her sister as she devoted her entire mind to finding a lucrative way of extricating their father and themselves from their predicament. Regular employment was as useless as the convent for apart from the meagre emoluments and long hours of toil there was nothing she could do sufficiently well—except become a governess, for which she was too young and wholly inexperienced—and from whom could she obtain the necessary character?

Every avenue of thought ventured along came to the same hopeless end—her pitiful lack of wealth. Each morning she marvelled at finding herself yet alive and after breaking her fast would go riding, sometimes with Rebecca—when they would occasionally meet Mr Liddell trespassing upon his cousin's land—but more often alone, with only a servant as escort, when she was able to give licence to her ideas, and serious consideration to any means whereby she could come by her desires—legitimately, or otherwise.

CHAPTER FOUR

It would appear that Christina was not the only person to journey thither to Hampshire in the winter of 1764, hoping to find fame and fortune. It chanced that one of dubious character purported to have jumped ship at Portsmouth also arrived, some two months prior to our heroine—one destined soon to become the scourge of the entire county and the prime topic of conversation from tavern tap-room to servants' hall and drawing-room.

It was one morning three weeks later, whilst Christina was awaiting the saddling of her mare to venture upon her ride, that she happened to overhear a groom and postilion exchanging awe-inspired views upon the latest escapade of the notorious Black Dan, and laying odds against him being caught before Eastertide. The groom went on to relate the vastly magnified tales currently being rumoured about the highwayman's great feats of daring—making of him a national hero rather than the blackguard he was—which in turn fired Christina's imagination to its limits. Already the seed of her ingenious plan was sown, soon to be nurtured and brought to fruition and acclaimed as the perfect solution to her problem— namely, Highway Robbery!

At first she was horrified with herself for even giving credence to the thought, and began to believe the Marquess's evil influence responsible. But the more she thought about it the less shocking it seemed to be, and the more enthusiastic she became, appreciating the distinct advantages of playing the female counterpart of Robin Hood. The extravagantly rich would never miss a trinket here and there; and she would certainly not harm anyone.

A week lapsed which Christina spent at variance with her conscience, arguing points for and against her plan— but mostly for—laying emphasis upon the rich benefits leading to her father's release, the re-purchasing of White-gables, and the pick of Society's handsome young bachelors for herself and Rebecca. Moreover, she would adopt a good disguise and take every possible precaution; and with a stout loaded pistol in her hand what had she to fear? No one would ever find out—not even Rebecca. And she failed to see how she was placing her life in any greater jeopardy than at present, living under the guardianship of a suspected murderer.

Thus decided, the only obstacle to be overcome was the pistol. Apparel was no problem for she had old clothing belonging to her father which she had brought, with the intention of selling it en route to Hampshire, but had not realised an opportunity. For a mask she would tear a piece off her mourning petticoats and she could soon twist one of her hats into shape—which left only the pistol. This—as she did not own one herself—she would need to appropriate from somewhere . . . perhaps, one of the Marquess's coaches?

* * *

As every moment meant the difference betwixt life and death Christina wasted no time in arranging her first venture, and the following night saw her stealing down the servants' stairs and out to the stables. Before saddling her horse she turned to the coach-house which embraced an impressive array of equipages, all bearing the Stryde coat-of-arms—furthermore, all equipped with fully primed flintlocks in their holsters which was of more immediate interest to herself.

Consequently, she was soon galloping confidently along the road on her friendly roan with one of the Marquess's long-barrelled pistols tucked in the top of her somewhat tight-fitting breeches, laughing at her former apprehensions, and already planning the administration of the plunder she was sure to get.

However, her mien told a rather different tale on her return some hours later when she clawed dejectedly back to her boudoir and flung herself on the bed in despair. All she had achieved for her pains were wounds to her pride and mud-spatters on her clothes; but she refused to give up, and gave vent to her feelings by kicking boots into one corner and flinging hat and mask into another, to the accompaniment of unladylike cursing.

Even so, Christina awoke next day more determined than ever to make her brilliantly conceived and meticulously arranged enterprise succeed, and that night was off on another venture. This time, she met with a modicum of success—and upon the next three nights, making a total prize of forty-eight pounds thirteen shillings and two pence farthing, plus a collection of rings, fobs, watches and shoe-buckles. Upon the sixth night, however, she acquired an even bigger haul in relieving two wealthy dowagers of their jewels and purses, which, as the victims fell into a dead faint with fright, proved her easiest conquest to date. But, alas, Fate intervened.

She was standing by the roadside gloating over her booty as she crammed it into her breeches' pocket, when she was launched upon from behind by a cannon-ball of animal aggression—seized in a vice-like grip whilst hat and mask were torn from her head—and so brutally manhandled that she began to think it a lion escaped from a travelling menagerie.

Christina wrestled like the female of the species, her arms threshing the air like a windmill-sails, and scratching, biting, kicking at her adversary, who seemed to be something of an expert on handling wildcats, unfortunately, and coped admirably throughout not once losing hold —to her wilder agitation.

"L-Let me g-go, you beast!" she spat breathlessly, her strength beginning to wane. "H-How dare you lay hands on me—"

"I'll dare more than that, Mistress Hell-cat!" growled a masculine voice savagely; and before she knew what was happening a rough hand grabbed her by the hair, wrenched up her face, and a barbarous kiss was planted on her parted lips.

When she managed to struggle an arm free she promptly dealt him a resounding whack across his masked face—to have it just as promptly returned.

Christina's hand flew to soothe her inflamed left cheek. She was too stunned to say anything as she gazed up at an impenetrable black mask through which two mysterious eyes glinted down at her. No one, not even her father, had ever dared to strike her before—which left only one course of action. And whipping forth her pistol, she levelled it at him, none to steadily, with indignant hand; but had no sooner done so than she felt a stinging blow on her arm, then landed, a dishevelled heap upon the grass and her pistol—her sole tangible means of defence—was in his possession.

"You may, or may not, deem yourself a gentleman, sir," she panted in wrathful outrage, sitting up to rub her bruised parts. "Nevertheless, I am vastly shocked that one—even of your class—should sink to the depths of striking a lady!"

"I've never struck a lady in my life," he flung back, showing more interest in the pistol—which significantly bore the Stryde crest.

"My appearance may belie my words," she snorted, fists clenched. "But contrary to what you think, I have mingled with the nobility!"

"So have I—in Newgate."

"But I have blue blood in my veins!" she shouted, certain she had some somewhere.

"And I have the Royal Coat-of-Arms tattooed on my chest!" he shouted back, wholly unimpressed.

"Y-You are impossible!" she screamed, throwing caution to the winds and drumming heels and fists in the grass. "I've never had the misfortune to meet such a pig-headed, infuriating, abominable, ill-mannered monster in all my—"

Her words were cut short instanter as she was seized by the shirt-front and dragged bodily to her feet where he held her in no gentle manner with one hand, while the other pointed the Marquess's pistol at her head.

"Now, Mistress Quality!" he demanded ruthlessly. "What's your lay? What the hell are you doing here on my domain?"

For the first time in her existence Christina understood the true meaning of fear. It paralysed her from head to foot as the cold steel contacted her temple, her teeth chattering in sympathy—making intelligible speech extremely difficult.

"Y-Your d-dom . . . ain?" she stuttered valiantly. "Y-You mean, y-you actually own this p-piece of highway, st-stone by . . . st-stone?"

"It's known throughout the Brotherhood that it's mine by right—which nobody, male nor female, has dared challenge till now!"

"B-Brotherhood? . . . Wh-What B-Brother . . . hood?"

"Don't play the innocent with me, wench!" he bellowed, shaking her violently. "You must have heard of the great protectors of the Criminal World! They take a very grim view of having their code of conduct broken—"

"C-Code of c-conduct? . . . b-but I didn't know—I-I really didn't, I swear!"

"—for which the punishment is death!" he snarled, cocking the pistol and preparing to fire.

"No!" shrieked Christina hysterically, her past flashing before her eyes. "P-Please! P-Please, d-don't fire! Please d-don't k-kill me! . . . I-If you j-just . . . l-let me g-go, I p-promise faithfully . . . n-never to s-set . . . f-foot here again." She broke off to delve into her pocket, producing the valuables which she eagerly offered. "T-Take them—th-they truly belong to you . . . n-now will you l-let me g-go?"

The touching plea of this fair damsel would have melted many a stony heart as she gazed up with anguished appeal written across her pale features, lips trembling, and copper lights in her long dark curls gleaming 'neath the moon; but she was dealing with a hardened rogue who not only remained utterly unmoved, but showed a keener interest in the glittering contents of his hand.

Suddenly he glanced up, his eyes piercing her through the mask.

"Risking your neck for such paltry baubles?" he cried with disgust, flinging the booty back at her.

"Paltry?" she echoed, piqued, grabbling about the grass to retrieve her lost gems. "Wherefore paltry?"

"The whole lot wouldn't bring you more than eighty pounds!"

"Which is better than nothing! M-My need is quite desperate—a-a matter of life and death."

"Whose?"

"M-My father's! H-He's in the Debtor's Prison a-and I must rescue him! And there's also my sister and me—w-we aren't safe in our beds!"

"Females seldom are," he scoffed. "Why you more than any other?"

"Our g-guardian plans to m-murder us—"

"He *what?*"

Highwayman he might be, even so, Christina was quick to detect a note of aversion in his voice which she did not hesitate to take fullest advantage of, in the wild hope of awakening an element of sympathy in his callous heart.

"I—It's true—on my honour!" she gasped out. "H-He murdered his father—f-frightened him to d-death—o-or did he poison him? Anywise, whichever it was, he'll do the same to us unless—"

"You're lying!"

"No! No!—I-I swear!" she exclaimed, casting frantically about in her mind how much she ought to divulge to this stranger—ultimately rescued by the words of Charles Liddell. "Everyone knows about it; it's regular village gossip. Oh, sir!" she hurried on. "Y-You must now appreciate my dire need for money?"

"P'raps I do," he rasped. "But I do not appreciate your way of getting it!"

"W-Why not? It's the perfect answer to my problems, and exceedingly convenient," she protested, nervously backing away from him at the way he was eyeing her. "Please, won't you help me?"

"Don't worry, my girl; I'll help you," he promised, a dangerous glint in his eye as he tossed away the pistol and jammed his cocked hat firmly over his dark hair, which was tied severely back in a stiff pigtail queue. "In fact, I'll give you something which will benefit us both enormously—something I'm sure your guardian would firmly endorse!"

And before she knew what he was about, he had her in a humiliating position across his knee and was belabouring her over the seat of her breeches, wholly impervious to her screams, threats, and gesticulations. Not until he had soundly administered the punishment did he release her to repair to his horse whilst she stood tenderly caressing her nether-regions, speechless with rage.

"How-How dare you!" she exploded finally. "H-How dare you abuse me in such fashion! Treating me like a common tavern wench! You—low-born son of a—a—nobody! A trumped-up, coarse-grained gutter-brat who ought to be taught a less—"

Yet again was she seized in no uncertain manner and

propelled—her feet not touching the ground—across to a tree.

"Although your description is very colourful, I think you'll find this one"—here, her nose was brought into sharp contact with an official proclamation nailed to the trunk—"is more detailed!"

The notice thus literally under her nose, Christina had little choice but to read printed thereon:

A REWARD OF 500 GUINEAS

will be paid to any Person or Persons giving Information leading to the Capture of one, Black Dan, notorious Terror of the Hampshire Highways—

DEAD OR ALIVE

DESCRIPTION

Is of Slender Build and Goodly Height. Wears own Hair (Brown) in Tarred Pigtail. Has Swarthy Complexion with badly scarred Forehead and Left Cheek.

IF YOU CAN HELP APPREHEND THIS DANGEROUS SCOUNDREL IT IS YOUR DUTY AS A LOYAL CITIZEN SO TO DO

Her eyes remained glued to the notice, digesting every word, oblivious of all—even her humiliating experience of a moment ago, and the fact that he had released her. But if Black Dan expected this alarming information to discourage her from her objective he grossly underestimated the tenacity of the female he was dealing with for conversely it filled her with a burning admiration.

"So you're Black Dan," she breathed awe. "I-I can't believe it! I've never met a wanted criminal before—certainly not one so famous. I'll warrant you've had some wild adventures!" she added, on a note of envy.

"You may now get on your horse and gallop back to your pedigree stock and boast, over tinkling teacups, of the badly needed thrashing I gave you."

Christina knew full well that she would never again be quite so fortunate and that she ought to take his sound advice before he changed his mind, and outstrip the wind to Barrington Hall, singing praises to heaven all the way for her deliverance from this murderous blackguard. Alas! not only did she choose to ignore the wisdom of this action, but actually suffered a pang of disappointment at being thus dismissed.

"Y-You want me to go?" she faltered, the despondency in her voice quite apparent, which evoked a peculiar look from him.

"Haven't you learnt your lesson?"

She turned away to hide her confusion, busying herself in seeking the errant pistol.

"I don't think you're all bad, Black Dan," she opined gently.

"And who are you to judge?" he flung at her over his shoulder. "Mayhap you find me in lenient mood."

"A very . . . lenient mood?" she probed cautiously.

"Now what's churning round in that distempered brain of yours?"

Christina paused, her conscience battling unceasingly to convince her that what she was about was foolhardy and dangerous, but to no avail.

58

"D-Do you frequent your highway every n-night?"

"Why should you be interested?"

She bit her lip, flashing him wary glances. "I-I just wondered—er—if you would perhaps consider . . . l-lending it to me," she suggested timidly, "—only one night a week—when you weren't wanting to use it yourself, of c-course."

Christina braced herself at his loud intake of breath.

"You're a determined baggage, aren't you?" he exclaimed in astonishment. "I take it you're going to pursue your crazy ambition, knowing you could finish up with a ball in your in'ards or your neck stretched?"

"Yes!" she replied stubbornly. "If not on your piece of highway, then on someone else's—someone who might not think twice about putting a ball in my—er—in'ards."

"You think that bothers me?"

"Why should it?"

Again she suffered misgivings as he advanced slowly, menacingly, towards her.

"And what do you think your guardian would say?"

Christina shivered at the very suggestion.

"What's to stop me making you rob your fine-feathered lord to guarantee my silence?"

"L-Lord?" she prompted, her heart plummeting to the depths of her stomach, wondering how he knew her guardian happened to be a lord, and a fine-feathered one, to boot.

"I might know more than you think . . ." he murmured shrewdly, as if divining her thoughts, gazing down in evident enjoyment of her discomfort. "What would your mad murdering Marquess do, I wonder, if he discovered your little game?"

She gulped, realising he was issuing no empty threat—

and that he must have identified the crest on the pistol. "I-I can't bear to imagine . . . M-My life wouldn't survive the hour."

"Then why risk it? He's worth a tidy sum; you could easily do your thieving on the inside. He'd never miss a ring or two—"

"S-Steal from the Marquess!" she gasped, shocked, as if he had suggested she desecrate the tombs of the ancient Pharaohs. "I shouldn't dream of doing such a thing! How could I repay him in such a dreadful way when he has taken us into his home and given us a roof over our heads? Even if it does hang over us like the Sword of Damocles, it's more than anyone else has done."

He viewed her curiously awhile, head to one side. "If you suspect him of murder shouldn't you report him to the authorities?"

A cry of alarm escaped her. "Oh, no! I couldn't possibly do that! You see, he—er—hasn't actually . . . d-done . . . anything . . ."

"So! It's all based on hearsay, and your frenzied imagination?" he challenged on a note of scorn. "Satan's Death! I'm beginning to marvel at his self-control—"

"But you don't understand!" she exclaimed with fervour, seizing his arm to revive his flagging interest and detain him. "I really do need money to save my father! That part's true, at least, —a-and . . . and . . ."

"Well?"

"—and to a-attract a rich h-husband."

"Ah! now *that* I can understand."

"—for he has threatened—in all honesty, I promise— to marry us off to some vulgar penniless peasants, and if we refuse—then he'll probably kill us!"

"Perhaps I should blow your brains out here and now

and do us all a service," he sighed with resignation. "You're sure one night will do?"

"Very well, thank you," she acknowledged politely.

"The thrashing hasn't taught you much, has it?"

But contrary to his assumption Christina had learnt a great deal in the last half-hour—for instance, what she would do in future if she chanced upon another rogue not tolerant enough to acquit her with a mere spanking, forced to admit that, despite her pistol and valiant spirit, alone, she was somewhat vulnerable in this world of cut-throats and scoundrels. No sooner had this registered than she turned her sights upon Black Dan to regard him as the wildest asset to her scheme, and worked herself up into the sacred belief that he had actually been sent by Providence to aid her cause. Therefore, she decided to hazard all in one final throw—including her neck.

"D-Dan?" she ventured doubtfully, not knowing quite how he would receive her staggering proposal, as he prepared to take his leave. "W-Would you . . . ?" she broke off nonplussed, fidgeting non-stop with her hat. "I mean, couldn't we . . . er . . . be—"

"Now just a minute—don't go leaping your hurdles before the horse!"

"But think of the advantages!" she cried, bursting with enthusiasm. "If we became partners there would be far less chance of us getting caught. We could safeguard each other—and share the plunder—you having the bigger share, of course, this being your—er—domain. And far from being a burden to you, Dan, I could be an enormous help!"

He paused at this final statement and turned from mounting his horse to view her curiously.

"You could?—how?"

"Well, I could tell you about any rich persons travelling abroad that I hear of—"

"Spy on your guardian's friends, you mean?" he queried with interest.

"N-Not his friends, exactly," she corrected hurriedly. "He doesn't seem to have many of those—but he has lots of enemies—very rich ones!"

He fell pensively quiet, seriously weighing the matter, as if some aspect of it appealed to him.

"Hm—mm, I begin to see tempting possibilities . . ."

"A-And two of us would be less dangerous, wouldn't it?" she stressed eagerly, disregarding the fact that he had managed to safeguard himself quite successfully hitherto without her kind assistance.

"I—er—suppose it would," he acknowledged.

"Then you agree?"

"For one night a week, you say?" he reflected, leaning over his horse, idly contemplating the heavens—whilst she stood tensed, awaiting the vital verdict. "Very well," he agreed finally. "I'm willing—but on one condition . . ."

"Yes?"

"That not a breath of it passes your lips."

"Oh, no, Dan! Never! I shan't breathe a word—on oath!" she pledged devoutly, willing to stake her right arm if need be. "My lips shall be sealed to the death!" she chanted, recalling part of an oath-taking ceremony she had once witnessed. "Er—as you've made a condition, may I make one too?"

"I'll consider it."

"W-Well, as women curry no favour with the law, would you do likewise, and conduct our partnership man to man—equal rights for both? I promise you won't be bogged down with a helpless languishing female."

He smothered a smile as he at last mounted. "I can but try—though I may suffer the occasional lapse of masculine weakness."

This casual observation caused her considerable perturbation which she sought to conceal in the shadows before making prodigious bother of mounting her horse, prompting him to point out civilly that had she been female he would have gallantly assisted her, but as she was now a man she would have to manage as best she may.

A meeting was then arranged for the following Friday and Christina galloped off along the road for Barrington Hall, highly satisfied with the outcome of the night; but her spirits might not have felt quite so elated concerning the future had she been able to see the ominous smile curling the lips of her new accomplice, before he threw back his head and burst into a fit of spine-chilling laughter. And wheeling his snorting animal about, he set off in the opposite direction, plunging through the ghostly trees until both he and the echo of his ghoulish mirth were engulfed in the gloomy darkness of the forest.

CHAPTER FIVE

It was lacking twenty minutes to three next morning when Christina stealthily made her way up the servants' stairs and back to her room where she lit a candle and undressed for bed with her mind in a whirl—far too excited to feel the least bit tired. Not until she was into bed and comfortably settled did she draw forth her handkerchief with trembling hands, to deposit, with tender care, the glistening contents upon the satin counterpane and proceeded to view each gem in the flickering light, trying to estimate its worth.

But her attention could not dwell for very long on her ill-gotten gains without embracing her new-found partner, prompting her for the first time to question the pangs of conscience she was experiencing, and to wonder if she had not acted rather imprudently by plunging headlong into this dubious partnership with a notorious felon? After all, what had this Black Dan to gain by engaging one so incompetent for a partner? Furthermore, the Marquess was no fool. Should he ever discover her nocturnal ventures there was no doubt in her mind concerning the terrible price he would demand her to pay. Then what would become of Rebecca and her father? All might be well at present whilst the Marquess was away from home, but upon his return she would need to tread very, very warily.

Several times she was sorely tempted to confide all to Rebecca but managed to save the day by recalling her implicit promise to Black Dan and the dire fate which would be hers if she broke her word. The utmost secrecy was imperative if her plan was to succeed—and it would be sheer folly to jeopardise it now when all was going well, with almost six hundred and thirty pounds to her credit, and an accomplice bold and fearless of wide experience who would never let her down.

Nervertheless, throughout the following week—which dragged interminably by—Christina's steadfast faith in Black Dan began to fluctuate, at intervals suspicious thoughts invading her peace of mind; thoughts that he was carousing in the village taverns, laughing and jesting with his comrades from the Brotherhood about the artless wench he had met a few nights ago, who had begged him—him! the infamous Black Dan!—to be her partner in crime—and she the ward of the Marquess of Stryde, to boot! It now occurred to her how easily this could travel back to her guardian, and Christina castigated herself for being so naïve.

Consequently, it was not without some misgiving that she prepared for her first official meeting with the highwayman and descended to the stables upon the Friday in question to saddle her mare as usual and select another pistol—from my lord's berlin, upon this occasion, and which would be replaced upon her return.

In her anxiety to please she arrived fifteen minutes early, though already of the firm conviction that he would not come—she unable to decide if she were delighted or saddened by the thought as she agitatedly shifted her weight from one booted foot to the other whilst keeping vigil by the tree displaying his 'wanted' notice.

But Christina did Black Dan a grave injustice, for he arrived promptly at the prearranged hour of eleven (when the wealthy were beginning to wend their divers ways homewards 'neath the effects of intoxication) seemingly from the very bowels of the forest. And yes, now that he was there inspiring her with much needed confidence, she was forced to own a feeling of profound relief.

The highwayman lost no time in commencing her instruction, and her first lesson in High Toby procedure was to remain out of sight until the coat-of-arms could be detected upon the coach-panels—and if the vehicle bore no coat-of-arms then it was seldon worth risking one's neck for. No, she was not to assume a bold stance in the middle of the road for it was an open invitation to be shot through the head or trampled to death.

Howbeit, not only did Christina benefit from his wide experience but also his senses which she soon discovered were exceedingly well developed—especially his hearing—and he stopped short of a sudden in the middle of the lesson to cock an ear upon the breeze, his hands progressing instinctively to his gleaming pistol butts.

"What is it, Dan?" questioned Christina, for as yet she could hear nothing but the sighing of the light wind through the overhead leaves.

"Sh—Sh!" he silenced her. "Listen!"

Christina did as she was bid and listened, though it was

quite half a minute before she distinguished the low rumbling noise of a coach bowling along the road.

"Our quarry travels at high speed. Quickly—up on your horse!" he commanded, grabbing her by a handful of frock-coat and hoisting her into the saddle. "Be prepared with your barker cocked—"

"Barker?" she faltered, puzzled.

"Pistol," he clarified impatiently. "Aim at the driver, and fire if I give the word!"

Sure enough the conveyance—a light carriage drawn by a team of four—swept into the moonlight from behind a bend in the road, about a hundred yards away.

"Well, well—if it isn't our friend Viscount Colville. I wonder how my venerable lord happens to be abroad at this uncivilised hour?" pondered the highwayman, stroking his smooth chin with the long barrel of one pistol. "Come, comrade! Keep well behind me, and watch my methods closely. I promise you some rare sport!"

There was no time to raise objections, even had she wished. The coach was almost level with them when Dan goaded his mount into its path, rending the night with a shattering explosion from his left flintlock as he ordered the coachman to 'stand and deliver!'

In stark fright the team shied violently to the right, their eyes rolling round their heads as the coachman fought nobly to control them before the coach was dragged over on to its side, taking the occupants with it. Fortunately the initial foul blast of the gentleman's wrath was lost in the wild pandemonium which ensued, of the frenzied whinnies, threshing hooves, and noise of grinding, splintering wood as the offside wheels disintegrated in the far ditch.

At this stage Christina had little to fear from the coach-

67

man or his postilion for they were too preoccupied with their cracked heads and frantic animals—both human and equinal—to even heed her presence.

"Hang me from yonder oak if 'tis not a damsel in distress!" declared Dan, leaping from his horse—to Christina's amazement—and striding across to set the tangled mass of hoops, satins and laces upon the shapely legs emerging from their midst. "Permit me to assist you from the wreckage, ma'am," he bowed with a flourish, at the dainty feet of the fashionable, if dishevelled, beauty who lost no time in casting her coquettish blue eyes upon him in preparation to barter anything rather than the priceless diamonds about her slender throat. "I trust you have sustained no injury?"

"La, to nought but my dignity, audacious sir," she simpered.

"My humblest apologies," he went on, kissing her proffered hand, "but I was not to know your cattle would take such powerful exception—er—likewise your noble lord," he appended, as vociferous curses continued to emanate from the gentleman within the vehicle, and whose irate countenance emerged through the doorway at this point—a countenance defying all description except that it had seen many winters and was partially obscured by a liberally powdered bag-wig.

With much groaning and heaving his lordship finally managed to extricate himself unaided, and promptly stormed up to the cause of the mishap—until he was prevented from advancing any nearer by the muzzle of a pistol in his ribs, when he respectfully retreated three paces before verbally attacking his foe.

"What, in Satan's name, do you mean by wrecking my newest equipage? Standing us all on our heads? Stampeding my cattle?—and seducing my mistress before my very eyes?" he exploded in outrage, his fists itching to pulverise the highwayman, but lacking the physical strength to realise this burning desire. "I suppose you will now have the brazen-faced impudence to rob me?"

Dan bowed his acknowledgement. "That is my intention, my lord, or this entire farce would be to no purpose. Your valuables, if you please," he requested politely, but with thinly veiled menace. "You too, ma'am."

The alluring coquette uttered a cry of dismay and fluttered her soft white hands to convey extreme agitation and alarm.

"Oh, good kind sir, I pray you! I beg you to spare mine honour! Take my diamonds—my pearls—my beautiful satin gown—even my embroidered garter! But I implore you—"

"Cease your whining, you brothel spawn!" cut in the Viscount blisteringly—causing Christina to wince as she did her best to conceal herself behind Dan. "How can the rogue spare what you've never had in the first place?"

"At least he's a gentlman!" screeched back the female, her true colours in evidence. "Which is more than can be said of you!"

"I shall relieve you of your diamonds, ma'am, and your pearls," Dan intervened, condescendingly. "And shall deign to spare your honour, and your blushes, by allowing you to keep the gown."

Obviously the lady would have much preferred the arrangement to be reversed as she stamped her beslippered foot in annoyance and her carmined lips fell into a straight disgruntled line before both she and her companion surrendered their jewels and trinkets.

"I-I'll see you swing for this, you vile scoundrel!"

snarled my lord, seething with fury at the indignity he was unable to do much about. "I'll see you dangling from the highest gibbet in Christendom! Drawn and quartered! And your entrails scattered—"

"Stow your gab in front of the lady!" Dan silenced him with a warning jab at the centre button of his waistcoat.

"Thank you, brave sir," inveigled the garish female, naturally assuming him to be referring herself for there was seemingly none other present fitting the description. "La, you must allow me to show my gratitude in the only manner I know"—and throwing herself bodily into Dan's arms she pressed her lips to his in a kiss of wildest abandon, as her male companion scowled on in the blackest resentment.

But his scowl was no blacker than Christina's who, for the first time in her life, was experiencing a powerful emotion of her own, an emotion she certainly did not relish, namely—jealousy; jealousy, at the way in which Dan was evidently enjoying the female's wanton overture—though why she herself should be tormented with such a feeling she was unable to fathom. But for her own condition in wishing to be treated as his equal, Dan would kiss her whenever she deigned to permit him. Had he not done so upon the night they met? Yes, but nothing like he was kissing this common woman of the town!

Indeed, it seemed a veritable age before Dan finally released himself from the woman's cloying arms and, remounting his steed, turned to thank the two for their generosity, doffing his hat in farewell as he urged his horse into action. And with Christina following on his tail, disappeared into the forest, leaving the couple to settle their differences in foul-mouthed abuse.

As Lord Colville's coach was not the only vehicle to be

waylaid that night by Dan and Christina, the sum total of their plunder exceeded eight thousand pounds which they divided equally, as agreed. This made Christina bitterly ashamed of having doubted him and she now deemed herself unbelievably fortunate to have found such a companion—certain that she never could have acquired so much on her own.

During the weeks which followed, she was further delighted to find that her partner not only kept faith with her, but abided strictly by the code, acknowledging her equality at all times, with the result that she found herself looking forward more and more each week to her trysts with the reckless highwayman, growing to trust him as she would indeed a brother, and priding herself on her judgement of character.

But that was not all. What delighted her even more was to find him a never-ending source of surprise. Sometimes he would dig in his heels and shout at her to race him through the forest, when they would gallop for all they were worth, as if the parish constables were indeed on their tails. Then, at other times, he would astonish her even further by producing a pair of rapiers and embark upon a fencing lesson, stressing how essential it was that she be able to defend herself in all eventualities. And if he was not making her gasp at his daring, he was evoking her hearty laughter at his infectious wit. Indeed, his vibrant person left her bereft of speech! And although nought in the world would have urged her to confess it, Black Dan had already swept her clean off her dainty booted feet.

All continued well for some considerable time until one night when her accomplice failed to appear, which served in no small measure to bring the fomenting situation to a climax. At first, Christina was not unduly perturbed as he was quite unpredictable, turning up all at once and taking her unawares; but an hour later she was nurturing doubts, though consoling herself in the knowledge that he had been detained for some innocuous reason. Perhaps his horse had cast a shoe? However, two hours later she was in acute agitation, and by the time the third hour had dragged by she was quite beyond herself. As it was now obvious he would not be coming, she reluctantly wheeled round her mare and set off homewards, her head in a turmoil. Intermittently, she cast hopeful glances over her shoulder, half-expecting to see the now familiar figure; but everthing remained dark and deserted, with the occasional screech of an owl to jar on her nerves.

It was now that the doubts gnawing at her heart flooded in and her imagination ran riot. The law had caught up with him! He was shot and lying wounded—even dying—somewhere! He had been press-ganged into the King's Navy! Or just got bored with their unconventional partnership—which she had to admit was rather unusual.

Although Christina expended the ensuing week in torment, yet did she stubbornly refuse to acknowledge these early pangs of emotion tugging at her heart, assuring herself that the feeling was no more than one friend would feel for another, and even went to the trouble of inventing an attack of megrims to divert suspicion at Barrington Hall. By the time Friday arrived she felt that she had aged twenty years, and spent most of the day closeted in her room on pretext of her 'megrims' lest her uncontrollable restlessness be remarked.

That night, her long-suffering was rewarded with the appearance of Dan himself, robust of health and without as much as a scratch in evidence, and who—to her torrid indignation—did not seem to think that any explanation was called for. Not wishing to look foolish, she merely smouldered to herself and decided to let the matter pass. But needless to say, their relationship following this minor difference was never quite the same, for Christina now realised how little she knew about him; what he looked like, where he lived, what he did during the days and nights they were apart, or even if he were married with a dozen children. This resulted in a bombardment of questions about his personal life when next they met—to which her accomplice took strong exception.

"Typically female!" he exploded with exasperation.

"They want to possess a man's soul the moment they feel their security threatened! You begged me to treat you like a man and I'm treating you like one. I'm the same with all my friends. We come and go as we please, as individuals—not chained together like convicts. It makes no difference to them what I look like or what I do with my time, so why should it to you? Why?"—he clapped a hand over her mouth as she made to reply—"I'll tell you why!" he went on, "—because you're a woman!—every ounce of flesh and bone as nature intended. You can smother yourself from head to foot in male garb, but you will still be what you are—an infernal, cozening, bewitching, tantalising, damned inquisitive female!"

A stony silence followed this outburst ere Christina summoned courage to probe with caution: "B-But if you were arrested and thrown into prison, Dan, how should I know? I shouldn't recognise you even if I met you face to face on visiting day."

"And why should you lose sleep over that?"

Christina held her peace, searching feverishly for the right words. "I-I'd m-miss you . . . I n-need you—"

"All you need is a half-wit to help you gather a fortune to gull some flush cove to the altar!" he flung back disparagingly.

"Th-That's not true!" she contradicted resentfully. "I agree I've grown to depend on you somewhat, but not for any ulterior reason. I-I like you a-as . . . as . . . a friend—and it is a normal human instinct to want to see one's friend's face."

He turned abruptly away, deeply disturbed at her words, not trusting himself to speak until he had regained control of his feelings.

"It is a human instinct you must needs forgo," he responded, almost inaudibly. "I can never unmask—for your protection as well as my own—"

"Y-You don't think I'd betray you?"

"You misunderstand. . . . What I have to hide would disillusion and horrify you."

Christina caught her breath as the words on the proclamation swirled round in her mind—'badly scarred forehead and left cheek . . .' She had heard tell of instances when swords and pistols were replaced by deadly acids, thrown in the aggressor's face as an alternative means of retaliation. Had Dan been one of these unfortunates?

Bravely and penitently she approached her forbidding partner.

"I'm sorry, Dan. I didn't mean to spoil everything between us. . . . Please don't be angry because I was a little thoughtless . . . I-I'm not very discreet sometimes. I'm sorry for being a female . . . a-and for being tantalising and inquisitive, and . . . and . . . c-coz . . . coz—what was it?"

"Cozening."

"Cozening? What's cozening?"

"Using your womanly wiles to unfair advantage."

Outrage choked Christina. "H-How can you accuse me of such a thing? Name one instance when I have been guilty of it! When did I ever throw myself in your arms like a certain female I could mention? Have not we always been equal? As true Brothers of the Road! Really, Dan, I see nothing to smile about. If you wish to submit another of your conditions, then do so!"

"Christina," he opined, lounging across his saddle, idly chewing a blade of grass, his tension banished. "You realise that this partnership cannot last for ever?"

Something tightened inside Christina, constricting her breathing. This was the moment she had long-dreaded, and hoped and prayed would never come.

"Eventually you will have enough wealth for your needs, when you will want to marry and settle down with the rich handsome nobleman of your choice."

Christina would never be more grateful to the moon for choosing this moment to pass behind a cloud, sparing her distress from his view. She was so confused! Why was it, that the thing which had been her most ardent desire only a few months ago now hung about her heart like a tombstone?

CHAPTER SIX

It was to be discovered at this time that the older girl was not alone in experiencing dramatic emotional changes wrought by the opposite sex. Christina observed, with a degree of sisterly curiosity, an even greater transformation in Rebecca who blossomed forth overnight into the sophisticated beauty she was destined by nature to be, as if suddenly aware of her true worth, and prepared to trade herself for nothing less than her heart's most ardent desire. She was not nearly so talkative—indeed almost as withdrawn as her sister—as if cherishing some deep dark secret to her bosom which no one, not even her confessor, would drag from her under the most exacting measures, and oft-times Christina would chance upon her rapt in a day-dream by the windows, with a half-smile playing round her rosy lips.

However, it was late one afternoon when Christina had been visiting Bob Milton's family that she returned on horse to Barrington Hall in company with her maid,

Molly, to be met by a very distraught Daisy Bigsley who expressed the utmost concern for her mistress, for apparently Rebecca had galloped mysteriously off in great haste without any escort.

Although Christina did not relish the thought of her young sister riding off alone, she nevertheless could not see any particular reason for Daisy's hysterics. Granted, Rebecca had been gone over an hour, but if she had intended riding to Withey Hill as Daisy unceasingly tried to impress upon her, then it would take a good half-hour to get there. Though why Becky should wish to visit such a desolate spot so urgently Christina was at a loss to understand, until Daisy revealed, in hushed tone, that Miss Rebecca had received a *billet-doux* from no less a person than Mr Wilde, suggesting a rendezvous at the place mentioned.

Christina accepted this news with an element of relief, but considered it rather unusual for Anthony Wilde to act in this clandestine fashion, he who was nothing if not the epitome of gentlemanly conduct, and at perfect liberty to rendezvous with Rebecca in the gardens of Barrington Hall any time he chose, without exerting himself to such a degree. Howbeit, she was prepared to concede that pressures of the heart affected some gentlemen in peculiar ways, and perhaps Mr Wilde wished to ensure that his privacy with her sister would remain inviolate.

She was in the midst of debating the propriety of Rebecca entertaining a gentleman unattended when Daisy delivered the crucial blow—that Rebecca was not with Mr Wilde at all.

"Not with Mr Wilde?" queried Christina, appreciation of Daisy's extreme anxiety hovering behind her confusion. "B-But I thought you said. . . . H-How can you be sure?"

"Because Mr Wilde is upstairs . . . i-in the G-Green Saloon, Miss Ch-Christina," lamented the stricken Daisy, "a-at this v-very . . . moment."

"What!"

"H-He arrived a few m-minutes ago . . . alone! A-And he cannot have c-called to s-see . . . his l-lordship, for *he* w-went out b-before . . . M-Miss B-Becky."

Christina did not care to admit to the conclusions her mind was now leaping to, and tried to obliterate them with logic.

"But he might have excellent reason for being alone, Daisy. Perhaps your mistress returned earlier without your knowledge?"

"N-No, miss—it's not p-possible! I have but just come from Miss Becky's room a-and—"

"All the same, we shall go up and enquire of him—"

"No, ma'am!" burst in Molly at this point, forgetting her place in the heat of the moment. "You must take care—great care, Miss Christina! I am worried for your own safety. Mr Wilde is a very close friend of . . . of . . . m-my lord. . . ."

"Yes? Well?" prompted Christina curiously. "Come, Molly—you may speak out."

But Molly was overcome with diffidence as she threw her mistress doubtful looks, fidgeting with the strings of her linen cap.

"D-Don't you see, miss?" breathed Molly—out of Daisy's hearing. "I-If Miss Becky's disappearance has—"

"But we don't know yet that she has disappeared, Molly!"

"Well, if she has, ma'am, and it has anything to do w-with—with—L-Lord Stryde, then Mr Wilde could be a—a—"

"Conspirator?"

Molly nodded in eager agreement.

Christina was ready to own the supposition a plausible one, yet found it difficult to accept that Anthony Wilde could be a willing party to the deception, being such a paragon of virtue and everything the Marquess was not. Indeed, one would have been sorely pressed to find a more incongruous pair. But Molly could be right. Nothing was to be gained by questioning Mr Wilde in anywise, for if he chanced in truth to be implicated in the Marquess's plot then she could hardly expect him to confess it openly; and if he was not, then it was reasonable to suppose he would know nothing whatever of Becky's misfortune which would be of little use and merely waste time she could put to better purpose in looking for Becky.

So, without further delay, Christina sent Daisy indoors with a few words of consolation and set off with Molly to find the straying Rebecca.

It would be a little after six o'clock when they reached Withey Hill—an eerie spot even in daylight, which made Christina shiver involuntarily and draw her cloak more tightly about her despite the autumn sunshine, hoping their search prove fruitful before darkness fell. Christina sat up erect in the saddle, straining her eyes round the surrounding countryside—the open fields to the left, and the coppice to the right, but not a glimpse of Becky was to be seen, nor even a cottage whereat she might enquire. Twice she called out to be rewarded with nought but the echo of her own tremulous voice; and so she suggested Molly search the coppice whilst she galloped round the hill to see what lay on the other side.

Thus, the search began, but had not progressed far when a shriek erupted from Molly, summoning her mistress to the coppice in all haste, there to find tethered to a tree, a horse placidly champing the grass—and unmistakably Becky's dapple-grey.

Christina uttered a cry of dismay, for until then she had harboured a degree of scepticism for Daisy's story which she had been about to dismiss as a flight of a young girl's fancy, preferring to believe her own intuition that Becky had diverted along another road to Barrington Hall and was safely back in her room, sewing samplers. But the sight of the grey banished these cherished hopes and confirmed Daisy's tale irrefutably.

The two girls continued the search, but now in extreme earnest, a race against the dusky shades of night looming in the east as the glorious evening sun sank in the west. Despite Molly's devout asseveration that she had scoured the coppice from end to end, Christina was about to insist they search it together, when the girl drew her attention to an old disused building perched way up on the summit of the hill, and which was so brightly illuminated by the sun that Christina wondered why she had not noticed it herself. As this appeared to be the only place left unsearched, maid and mistress tethered their mounts alongside the grey and promptly set off uphill afoot—as it was rather steep. Christina's flagging spirits were stimulated again for it seemed a perfect place for a rendezvous, and she hoped in her heart that she would find Becky with nothing more serious than a twisted ankle—refusing to give credence to the improbable thought that her sister might have eloped or been abducted for there was no evidence whatsoever of another horse having been there, let alone a coach and four.

From some three hundred feet below, the old barn looked innocuous enough, but the further Christina climbed the greater waxed her apprehension and less welcoming looked the barn. She carefully picked her way along the narrow winding path which now led her round to the eastern side—to find the rays of the dying sun throwing the barn's irregular contours into bold black relief, giving it an almost sinister appearance.

She shrugged the feeling aside, convinced that it was nothing more than an optical illusion; yet she shivered again as the evening breeze graduated to a wind, and the darkness crept menacingly up behind.

But up at the barn she found the atmosphere more uncanny than ever, as if the sinister air rose up the hillside to culminate at the barn itself, which seemed positively to exude evil. Indeed, a more austere-looking place Christina had never seen in her life, and her present instinct was to turn and flee down the hill as fast as she was able, but this her inborn curiosity and concern for Becky forbade . . . or was it the barn? Despite her revulsion she found it drawing her mysteriously, as if she must look inside at all cost—even of her life! She could feel Molly trembling close behind and, appreciating that the responsibility of entering lay with herself, she cast an eye vainly over the exterior for sight of a window, then stepped bravely forward, calling: "Becky? A-Are you in th-there?" in a quivering voice—which met with a deathly silence.

She took the final hesitant steps up to the forbidding door, though it is questionable if she would have taken them at all had she known that Molly was backing cautiously away, with the obvious intention of deserting her mistress in this, her hour of dire need. As Christina timidly pushed the door it unleashed a shriek of agony and she leapt back, trembling with fright, only to creep forward again, gingerly pausing on the theshold and peering anxiously round the dim musty interior, crying out again: "Becky? B-Becky?"—when with a sudden gasp, she spied a pair of booted feminine feet protruding from a riding-habit of black bombasine.

"Becky!" she exclaimed, rushing through the door—to be brought down by a fell blow on the back of her head, dealt by an unseen force. Christina dropped on the spot, to be roughly dragged across the hay to lie alongside her sister, where she was left by the mysterious black figure, who emerged from the barn, firmly locking the door before setting fire in hot pursuit of the panic-stricken Molly.

*   *   *

How long she had lain unconscious Christina—when she eventually stirred—was unable to estimate, but it did not take very long to register in her throbbing head how she came to be where she was and the circumstances appertaining to it. With a groan, she sat up in the inky blackness, administering a tender hand to her swollen head, impervious to the rats scampering about her feet, and the fetid smell to which she was rapidly becoming accustomed.

Having rallied her senses she sat quite still, listening for a sound—any sound, but everything remained unnaturally quiet except for the scuffling of the rats and faint howl of the wind outside. She struggled to her knees and began to grope about in the hay for Becky, calling loudly as she grew more and more alarmed—for there was not even a sound of breathing—until she groped about on the other side, soon to locate the prone body of her sister. Thankful to find her breathing, even though it was rather faintly, she shook her gently.

"Becky—Becky!" she cried yet again, to meet with no response.

Her next, and arduous task, was to find means of escape as quickly as possible, for whoever was responsible for imprisoning them therein would no doubt return in due course. Again she searched about in the darkness—this time for some heavy implement, for the walls and door were much too solid to penetrate with her own bare hands—eventually to chance upon a rusty pitchfork, which shattered into pieces upon its first sharp impact with the door.

Christina did not relinquish hope, and again searched—for something a little more robust—hoping that when they did finally get free their horses would still be where they had left them, tethered in the coppice.

Even so, despite using every means at her disposal—and several more that the average female would not have thought of—Christina found herself still firmly imprisoned. Having hacked and chopped, kicked and shouted for help untill she was hoarse she was now utterly exhausted and resolved to await her fate mutely, when an unexpected sound outside caught her sensitive ear, and she sat up to listen intently, detecting quite distinctly the sound of someone moving about outside the barn, who would not seem to be their gaoler, for whoever it was, was not making any attempt to disguise his presence, if the thuds and bangs against the walls were aught to go by.

Christina immediately rallied her remnants of breath and shouted as lustily as she could, bethinking someone had come to investigate if there were anyone inside the place, but alas! her judgement could not have been more at fault as a most unpleasant and ominous odour assailed her nostrils.

"S-Smoke!" she gasped in horror, before a flame

sprang to life through the bottom of the door, to be joined by another, and another, leaping up the walls in great voracious tongues to devour everything in reach, brilliantly illuminating the smoke-filling barn and the two doomed girls. Rebecca was still unconscious, now with little chance of ever waking, and Christina was thundering for help upon the walls, hammering with her fists and scratching with her fingernails until they were broken— screaming out for all she was worth till, overwhelmed with fumes, she sank, choking, to her knees as the flames licked within feet of her petticoats, then inches—growing hotter and hotter, ready to engulf her—when there was a deafening crash followed by splintering wood as part of the rafters and a wall fell in, and Christina felt herself swept aloft in strong masculine arms and borne out into the fresh night air and laid to rest upon the soft grass.

There she lay, coughing, gulping in lungfuls of air, marvelling how she had been suddenly spirited out of the blazing inferno to safety whilst listening to the wood crackling as the barn slowly crumbled to ashes—and the footsteps of her heaven-sent deliverer as he hastened back and forth. Forcing up her head, she blinked her smarting streaming eyes to distinguish a blurred shape, black, bending solicitously over the prostrate figure of Becky; then she was seized by a fit of violent coughing, and fell back to bury her scorched face in the cool, cool grass ... until raised again in those same strong arms, but this time infinitely gentle, and her aching head cradled on a comforting shoulder; then peering up through the mist shrouding her eyes, found herself staring into the masked face of her highwayman.

"D-Dan?—I-Is it really you?" she stammered, bemused.

"Who else would be at hand to rescue you from your folly, Christina? And at such risk to life and limb? Satan's Death, girl!" he swore vigorously. "How the devil did you get in such a mess? It was a sheer miracle that I happened to be in the area."

"I-I—" she broke off, and in evidence of her ecstatic joy—burst into tears.

He did not pursue the question but instead held her close, resting his face on her hair, allowing her to give licence to the emotional turmoil comsuming her, as she clung to him, desperately, unable to believe that he was there—her Black Knight—arriving in the stroke of time to save her from the jaws of a terrible death.

"B-Becky?" she sobbed brokenly. "I-Is she . . . ?"

"A little drowsy, but she should be all right."

Christina looked across in anxiety at her sister who was giving support to his words with a cough or two.

"And yourself?" he went on. "Are you well enough to tell me what this is all about? And how, in heaven's name, you come to be roasting alive out in this wilderness at one in the morning?"

She inhaled a deep breath and gasped out: "B-Becky . . . received a m-message . . . f-from a cer . . . tain g-gentleman . . . t-to meet him h-here." She fell again into a coughing fit, then continued, "I-I c-came . . . l-looking and f-found . . . her unconscious . . . in there . . . th-then some . . . thing hit m-me. I h-heard some . . . one outside . . . I-I thought w-we . . . were being r-rescued . . . then I s-smelt . . . smoke a-and we w-were . . . on f-fire—"

"Christina! Are you certain of this?" he cut in sharply. "You haven't been up to mischief again? Or dreamt it?"

This had an instant sobering effect upon her and she bobbed up with a spark of her customary spirit.

"Dreamt it!" she ejaculated. "When I have a lump the size of a duck's egg on my head to prove it? And you think I came all this way to set myself on fire by accident?"

"No, but if what you say is true," he pointed out—deep concern registering in his voice which helped compensate in abundant measure for all she had suffered, "and this night's work was deliberately planned, then obviously someone has a rabid ambition to see you dead."

"At least we are finally agreed on that point!"

"Ye gods, girl! You don't still imagine the Marquess—"

"I imagine nothing of the sort. It is simply sound reason, Dan, for he is the only person with motive and opportunity, and furthermore, who knows of Becky's penchant for Mr Anthony Wilde—apart from Mr Wilde himself, who assuredly would not resort to such chicanery with all the motive in the world."

"But why should he go to such ridiculous lengths when he could easily have you made away with in some secluded corner of his estate? Pushed from a high window? Or buried in his orchard and claim you'd returned to Yorkshire?"

"And run the risk of being discovered? Apart from accomplices whom he would need to trust implicitly. No," went on Christina, glancing round her with a shudder, "this place would suit his purpose to perfection, where he could commit his dastardly deed undisturbed, and unseen."

"A blazing barn would scarcely pass unseen," he enlightened her with fervour. "It certainly caught my eye. I'll warrant it could be seen five miles away, though I didn't realise there was anyone inside, least of all you, until I got near enough to—"

"C-Chris . . . tin . . . a . . ." wailed Rebecca at this stage, arresting attention to the exclusion of all else.

"Becky!" exclaimed Christina, fleeing to her sister's side, where she lay snugly enveloped in Dan's thick surtout. "I'm here, dearest. What happened? Can you tell me?—H-How do you feel?"

Becky fluttered open her eyes, gazing at her sister as if she had never set eyes on her before, then at the highwayman towering behind—who did not seem to startle her at all—then back at her sister again.

"Christina?" she probed plaintively, as if doubting if it truly were she. "W-Where am I?"

"Don't be afraid, Becky; you are quite, quite safe," Christina reassured her, chafing her hand. "This gentleman is a friend, and is going to look after us."

Becky's blue eyes shuttled betwixt Christina and the highwayman as if having difficulty in reconciling the two.

"Becky, you must tell me all you can remember. I know you came to meet Mr Wilde, but what happened when you got here?"

Tears welled up in Becky's eyes and coursed down her cheeks.

"M-Mr Wilde w-wasn't . . . h-here . . . i-it was s-some . . . one else. . . ."

"Who, Becky? Who?" breathed Christina in a frenzy of suspense.

"I-I don't . . . know . . . i-it was d-dark . . . h-he g-grabbed . . . m-me . . . I struggled . . . th-then something h-hit . . . m-me . . . D-Daisy? Wh-Where's . . . Daisy?"

"Daisy is safely at Barrington Hall, where we shall all be directly," comforted Christina, trying gently to prise open her sister's tightly clenched fingers—nurturing suspi-

cions she had some object contained within—to find sure
enough, a ring of some considerable value.

Christina sprang to her feet, urging Dan to accompany
her over to the devastated barn, where in the light of the
glowing embers they examined the ring closely.

Suddenly Christina emitted a loud gasp. "L-Look, Dan!
I-It bears an inscription!"

"Hm-m . . ." he pondered. "Something 'B'. . . ."

" 'V'! It must be 'V'! Don't you see? 'V' for Valentine—Valentine Barrington, Marquess of Stryde! Now do
you believe me? Now, do you understand?"

The highwayman's lips tightened in a murderous line.

"I most certainly do," he murmured ominously,
"—without any doubt!"

Christina dragged her eyes from the ring she held to
view him oddly, for his words—but more his manner—
would seem to constitute a veiled threat. And his next ut-
terance did nothing to dispel this qualm.

"Do not underestimate your enemy, Christina," he ad-
jured her grimly. "Never forget that he is as wise as you
yourself—if not wiser. He will remember when and where
he lost his ring; moreover, that you may identify it. Take
solemn warning. Do not overplay your hand, for next
time, I may not happen conveniently by."

Panic gripped her at the note of finality in his voice.

"Dan—y-you sound strange . . . W-We will meet as
usual, next F-Friday's eve?"

His hesitation seemed to be interminable. "Fret not, I
shall come. But the day is not far distant when we must
part company, and go our divers ways—"

"G-Go? Where will you go?" she gasped anxiously.
"Won't you always be there, on your domain?"

He shook his head decisively. "I have become too notorious in the area. Perhaps, I shall go abroad awhile, till the hue and cry has died down. You see now, Christina, why 'tis better you know nothing about me? I cannot be unwittingly betrayed."

"A-And I shall n-never ... see you ... again?" she faltered miserably.

"Alas, no."

Even now, at this eleventh hour, Christina could not acknowledge herself in love. Love, she had always believed to be a happy emotion, when one was so delirious with joy that one wanted to cry for the sheer pleasure of it—not the agony of heart and soul she now experienced, with a great aching void inside her. True, she had never felt more like crying in her life; but it was certainly not due to pleasure.

CHAPTER SEVEN

Although Christina extracted promises on sworn oath from her young sister to make no mention of what had happened, word somehow got abroad of their terrible ordeal—which she succeeded in convincing everyone had been sheer misfortune. Nevertheless, Rebecca did hearty justice to their miraculous rescue, only just managing to stop herself blurting out that it had been effected by none other than a highwayman—for which her sister truly would never have forgiven her—and so simply stated that the role had been played by a chance passer-by.

Everyone expressed extreme anxiety, not least of all Molly Anders, with whom Christina was reasonably angry, but who was so abject in her appeal for forgiveness, upon bended knee, that Christina anon acquitted her with a mere scolding instead of the sound beating she deserved.

Everyone was anxious, that is, except the Marquess, who regarded the incident with an unnatural aloofness—which did not surprise Christina one whit, and served only to establish his guilt the more. This was contrary to her opinion of Mr Wilde who not only confirmed her former impression that he was innocent of any part in the business, but made a rapid ascent in her esteem (and still further in Rebecca's) by superabounding with concern, insisting they keep to their beds for a day or two and receive commensurate attention. It would seem the only acknowledgement my Lord Marquess intended granting was the imposing of a further command, namely, that his wards were not, in any circumstances, to ride unescorted, and they were to keep within sight of the house at all times; furthermore, if they broke this rule, they would be forbidden to ride altogether.

Therefore, Christina was pleasantly taken aback when she and Rebecca were unexpectedly summoned to their guardian's presence upon the fourth morning after the incident. As the two had exchanged no more than a dozen words with his lordship since the fatal night of their arrival, and this was the first official summons they had received from him, she did not see how it could possibly be for any reason other than to make a pretence at commiserating with their grave misfortune. Even so, there would seem to be little cause for Rebecca's wild elation at what could still prove a more gruelling experience than the fire itself.

And so, the two at length descended the stairs, Christina adorned in a saque dress of black taffeta trimmed with furbelows and spread over a wide farthingale, complemented by black ribbons in her hair, while Rebecca followed behind, her slim figure similarly attired but with her petticoats more modestly hooped.

Upon arrival at the study Christina tapped lightly upon the door which was instantly opened from within by the inevitable liveried footman, who obsequiously bowed them over the threshold.

The Marquess was seated near a window behind a huge ebony and tortoiseshell desk, his handsome face marred by a look of concentration centred upon the document clasped in his elegant white hands. As he was in second mourning, his exquisitely styled coat was the conventional black, but of brocade, and relieved by frothing white lace at chin and wrists, while his long black hair lay lightly confined in a wide black bow at the nape of his neck.

Immediately Christina's eye alighted upon him the same overawed feeling that she had first experienced began to creep over her—as if her bones were dissolving into jelly—and she swiftly transferred her trembling hands to her back lest he thus detect her discomposure. But Lord Stryde did not yet seem aware of their presence as his eye remained riveted to the document—an impression Christina endeavoured to preserve as she ventured cautiously up to the desk, with Rebecca tip-toeing behind, now not nearly so sure that what she had anticipated with eagerness would come to pass if the Marquess's expression was anything to go by.

Her sister's tension was apparent in the way she fidgeted with her handkerchief, but after waiting an appreciable time she grew bold enough to give a nervous cough or two in order to attract his attention. This ultimately met with a degree of success as, without averting his eyes from the document, he requested them to be seated—which prompted Christina to timorously enquire if the interview was likely to be a long one—an enquiry which was ignored, likewise the repetition of it, and so the two resigned themselves to relieving the suspense in their divers ways.

Anon, he set the paper aside and lounged back in his chair to view them thoughtfully, his steady calculating gaze generating a deep flush in Christina's hitherto wan cheeks, causing her to wonder how he had the audacity to sit there brazenly confronting her as if there were nothing more serious betwixt them than his superiority of wealth, position and intellect.

His pallid features harboured a hint of boredom as he idly picked up the bejewelled letter-opener to hand, with which he proceeded to pare his already well-manicured fingernails. In truth, before he even spoke his very demeanour would not appear to denote concern, and if Christina yet lived in hope of a lengthy peroration pouring forth overwhelming sympathy on her behalf she was due for a considerable shock.

"I asked you to be seated," he remarked casually.

"A-And I, my lord," pointed out Christina respectfully, "asked how long it is likely to take."

"That," he replied, with emphasis, "remains to be seen. But I shall expedite the matter by coming straight to the point and announcing that one of you is not destined to revel in the joys of spinsterhood very much longer. Ah!—I see you prefer to be seated after all," he appended as the two descended into the nearest chairs, Christina more by way of collapse.

"Wh-Which of us is so doom—I-I mean, destined?" she stammered fainly.

The Marquess gave way to a furtive smile. "Your sister, Miss Warsford; but despair not," he resumed swiftly, spiking her relief. "No doubt your turn will come in the not too distant future."

"M-Me?" wailed Rebecca, fleeing for refuge to her sister's comforting arms. "Y-You can't mean it! Y-You can't, m-my lord! You gave your word; you promised!"

"Promised what, Becky?" asked Christina, understandably confused.

But Rebecca continued addressing her remarks to Lord Stryde.

"You promised, y-your lordship, that if my feelings did not change in three months you would seriously consider—and they haven't! They haven't! I am seventeen now and much, much more mature, and my feelings are exactly the same! I've never been so sure of anything before in my whole life! I sw—"

"Becky!" broke in Christina, no wiser in spite of this long harangue. "What on earth are you gabbling about?"

Rebecca turned to gape at her as if the answer were perfectly obvious and that it was exceedingly obtuse of her sister not to appreciate what it was all about when every servant in the place had tittle-tattled of nothing else for weeks past.

The Marquess came to the rescue with a stifled yawn. "Your sister is endeavouring to convince me of her undying devotion to my dear friend, Mr Anthony Wilde."

Christina was somewhat bewildered, though she could scarcely own the news unexpected, especially when Mr Wilde's visits to Barrington Hall had been almost unceasing of late with no attempt on his part to conceal the reason; yet she had not realised that his affections (nor her sister's) were engaged to such a degree. Obviously she had been too preoccupied with her own affairs to notice what was happening under her very nose.

"A-And Mr Wilde?" she pursued, expectantly. "H-He reciprocates this devotion?"

"So I believe," her guardian murmured, more interested in the enormous sapphire adorning the middle finger of his right hand.

"Oh yes, Chris!" burst forth Rebecca in ardent support. "He does! He does!"

"Then forgive me, my lord, but why do you object to the match?" queried Christina of the Marquess, who heaved a sigh of strained forbearance.

"I was not aware that I had," he responded with admirable control. "If the pair of you will cease haggling and confusing the issue, you will discover that a contract of marriage is being drawn up and will be signed and sealed within the month, though the actual betrothal will not take place until some time after, allowing for the arrangement of some kind of celebration in honour of the occasion, you understand, and for the house to emerge from its official mourning."

A breathless hush greeted the disclosure.

"Y-You mean, Mr Wilde and I will be p-permitted to w-wed?" stammered Rebecca, anon.

"Why not? I suppose he's old enough to know what he's about; and it rids me of one millstone"—adding before she could fly into transports of joy and devour him with gratitude—as she looked about to do: "You may show your appreciation by, afterwards, fulfilling the terms of contract as soon as is decently possible."

His words were drowned beneath screams of delight as the two sisters hugged and kissed, Christina enraptured with the match, which seemed to auger well for her young sister's future, and which could only delight their father.

As the sound of rejoicing died away the Marquess flashed Christina a glance of despair, addressing Rebecca.

"Somehow I fear I shall not be rid of your sister quite so easily."

"But that's where you are mistaken, my lord!" bubbled Rebecca with renewed excitement.

"Becky—" tried to interrupt Christina.

"I'm not supposed to know anything about it! It's a deep dark secret!" she chirruped, clapping her hands in anticipation of the stunning effect her news was going to have and oblivious to the gaping trap she was setting for her sister. "You have no need to look for Christina a husband, my lord; she's already found one!"

A horrifed gasp escaped Christina as the Marquess suddenly assumed an interest—paper-knife suspended—his eyes, following the initial surprise, suffused with a mixture of curiosity and scepticism.

"Precisely how came you by your startling information?" he queried dryly.

"One doesn't need to be told, my lord; it's plain for all to see," declared Rebecca, glancing significantly at her sister, who felt ready to expire at any moment. "She's so hopelessly in love!"

"Is that all?" drawled the Marquess, flicking a speck of snuff from one huge cuff. "Mayhap, because you yourself are infected with the malady you imagine everyone else to be?"

"But it's as plain as the hump on a cottage-loaf! You must have noticed, my lord? Everyone else has. Besides, she must wed first or we'll be frowned upon by Society!"

"Becky!" cried out Christina again, now conscious that Rebecca spoke nothing more than the truth, yet obstinately wanting to gainsay it.

"Don't try to deny it, Chris. You've been baying at the moon like a love-lorn spaniel for weeks. Even Anth—I mean, Mr Wilde remarked it. After all, we should recognise the symptoms better than anyone." This struck her as extremely funny, and she lapsed into giggles.

But her sister did not find it at all amusing, and neither, apparently, did Lord Stryde, whose black brows drew together before he turned his inscrutable gaze full upon Christina, to find her heightened colour and pained expression abundantly proclaiming her guilt.

"And who, may I ask, is the object of this overwhelming passion?"

"Your Cousin Charles!" piped up Rebecca, obligingly.

Had Christina been gifted with sufficient foresight to anticipate the dire consequences of an impetuous tongue, the worst might have been avoided, and in circumspectly holding her peace thus acknowledged a situation which was bad, though not irremediable. Instead, she courted open disaster for which she was clearly headed. But alas!—to be accused of loving the wrong man was more than she could tolerate.

"It is not my lord's cousin!" she flared, rounding on her sister.

"It is! It must be! He's the only man you've met—"

"He is not the only man I've met!" shouted Christina furiously, one foot in her sister's trap.

"He is, Chris!" persisted Rebecca breathlessly. "Apart from his lordship here, the servants, and—" she stopped short, her round blue eyes agog upon Christina. "Ooh—can it be? . . . Ch-Chris—are you in l-love with the h-highwayman?"

The paper-knife clattered on the desk. "The *what*?" ejaculated the Marquess.

"Highwayman, my lord," submitted Becky dubiously, beginning to wonder how she had thought it such a good idea to divulge it in the first place as she witnessed her sister's suffering. "H-He rescued us f-from the b-blazing b-barn."

Christina sat rigid, eyes closed, gripping the arms of her chair as the whole room spun round and round.

"I-Is something wrong, Christina?" she faltered, wrenching the knife in her sister's wound. "H-Have I blundered?—I-I'm exceedingly sorry . . . I-I think I under- . . . stand . . . ."

The Marquess rose unhurriedly, and made his way over to where Rebecca stood contrite and forlorn, wholly unaware of the havoc she had wrought in the space of a few seconds.

"You have certainly blundered, child," he informed her kindly, placing a paternal hand on her shoulder and guiding her towards the door, "but I doubt vastly if you understand. I suggest you leave your sister and me alone awhile—'twould appear we have something to discuss."

With a rueful glance at Christina, Rebecca did as she was bid and retired without demur.

Lord Stryde dismissed the footmen and closed the door, to pause against it surveying Christina, re-assessing her in the light of this new evidence, as she sat opposite the great windows, staring straight ahead across the tops of the cypress trees and neat lawns which swept away into the distance, her hands tightly clasped in her lap testifying to her tense emotional state. At last, he transferred his attention to the japanned cabinet in the corner, his almost benevolent attitude of a moment ago now banished as he helped himself to the brandy.

Meanwhile Christina continued rallying together her forces for the fray which was to come, determined to reveal absolutely nothing likely to further endanger the life of the man, she now realised, she loved desperately.

"Well, Miss Wansford," he prompted eventually, "are we to play at guessing games? . . . As you will," he shrugged sauntering round the room glass in hand, to the soft rustle of his stiffened skirts. "This man—I am not sufficiently naïve to expect you to divulge his name." He hesitated as a vacant expression descended on her countenance. "You seem to labour 'neath some uncertainty. You are in possession of it, I presume?"

Her eyes fought to meet his, failed, and fell to her clenched hands.

"And are you equally conversant with his family and prospects?"

Christina saw no point in lying—aware, and inwardly rankled, that her face must be screaming the answer.

"May I boldly enquire if you know anything about your—er—highwayman lover?"

"He is not my lover!"

"But a highwayman, nonetheless," he stressed callously. "A ruthless bloodthirsty knave who will finally be drawn, hanged, disembowelled, then his remains tarred and strung up in chains as a deterrent to the rest of the community for—"

"No! No!" screamed she, unable to endure any more, leaping to her feet. "I won't let them! No one could be so cruel!"

"The law can be extremely cruel and beareth respect for none—man nor woman!" he rasped harshly.

"But he isn't just any ordinary felon," she deprecated passionately. "He is a good honest man who has been led astray by misfortune."

"And if he does evade the gallows, what has he to offer? Assuming he would be willing to offer it to you—

99

er—that is, if he hasn't offered it to someone else long ere this."

"Now what do you insinuate? That he is already wed?" she exclaimed resentfully, perhaps more annoyed that he had hit perilously near the doubt consuming her own heart. "How can you think such a thing—that he would be so deceitful—when you don't know him and haven't even met him? He isn't like that, my lord. You don't understand—h-he would have told me, I'm sure. W-We trust each other implicitly. He would never play such a shabby trick! Never!"

For one pregnant moment distraught green eyes managed to meet implacable black—until they wavered and fell.

"Faith, it's worse than I envisaged," he muttered, draining the glass which he continued to twirl in his fingers, frowning down at the flamboyant coat-of-arms of his family portrayed on the side.

Christina summoned some elements of dignity and reseated herself with a rustle of billowing petticoats, biting her lip as she inwardly rebuked herself for allowing him to provoke her so, determining that he was not going to panic her into divulging anything further. If she did begin to sense the four walls closing in on her, she was nevertheless, going to maintain her external calm. As yet, he knew nothing whatever about Dan, and if she kept a cool head the position need not alter.

"Am I to assume from all this that you would actually wed the man?" he questioned at length.

"Yes!—if he should ask me."

"A man with nothing to commend him?" he stressed, viewing her askance. "And your father—you think he would approve the union?"

Christina shuffled uneasily in the chair, nurturing misgivings.

"A-As my future happiness depends entirely upon it—yes."

"Even when 'tis doomed to disaster from the outset?" he sneered with disdain. " 'Tis indubitably through founding his own future upon such flimsy epithets that he finds himself in his present lamentable position—a bitter lesson his daughter would do well to heed."

Christina would have responded with an equally cutting remark had she not lacked the moral courage to do so, beneath the burning glare of his dark pitiless eyes. He hesitated, placing the delicate crystal upon a side-table with grave deliberation.

"I cannot stress too strongly my understanding of your unfortunate situation," he went on, in milder tone. "However, I intend to extricate you no matter—"

"But I don't want to be extricated! I am quite happy in my unfortunate situation!"

"This impossible relationship must cease—or I cannot be answerable for the consequences!"

Again Christina leapt from her chair. "You can't mean it ... You can't! Even you couldn't be so heartless, my lord!"

"Surely you have resided her long enough to know that I am seldom otherwise?" he rejoined acidly. "I am not given to fits of sentiment."

Emitting a groan, she turned away to hide the anguish manifest on her face only to turn back to him again, in earnest supplication—an attitude absurdly alien to her nature until this dire moment, aware that it would prove no arduous task for a man of his elevated status and cunning to have Dan snared and flung into prison before cockcrow.

"P-Please, my lord?—if-if he were to prove himself worthy?"

"It's out of the question."

"But if he were to give up his life of crime?"

"I am adamant!" he thundered conclusively, causing the windows to vibrate. "You must purge yourself of this reprobate once and for all, and the only way is to sever connections with him now before it is too late."

"Why? Why?" she besought him, wondering why he—with all his wealth and power at his command—would not wave his wand and grant her what she wanted more than anything in the whole world. "It is the perfect solution to both our problems—for I should be the happiest woman alive, and you would be disburdened of me for ever, which in turn should make you the happiest man, my lord, should it not?"

The Marquess seemed a trifle disconcerted. Rather odd, perhaps, for no man was more accustomed to the fair sex begging and supplicating for favours than he, but none with pale upturned face of such stirring beauty, eyes as green as the most priceless emeralds in his collection, long ringlets the colour of the maturest Burgundy wine in his cellars—ringlets which ran down a cream satin shoulder to end with a gentle caress upon the tempting rise and fall of two fully developed breasts protruding—palpitating—over the bodice of her gown.

"Aye—verily it should, Miss Wansford," he replied pensively anon. "Verily it should . . . however, as you are my responsibility you will marry someone respectable if it exhausts all my wealth and ingenuity in the process."

"Why should you be anxious about my impending ruin?"

"Not anxious, merely obliged to avert it," he corrected with sangfroid, meandering over to the window to gaze out with satisfaction upon all he commanded. "No matter what my relatives may allege to the contrary, my dedication to duty would do honour to a priest—when I set my mind to't. Anywise, how you can seriously contemplate holy wedlock with a man about whom you know absolutely nothing is utterly beyond my comprehension!"

"A woman doesn't need to know a man's life history to fall in love with him!" she parried acrimoniously. "But perhaps that is something the Marquess of Stryde would never understand!"

The Marquess rounded from the window, eyes narrowed. "Wouldn't I? Mayhap you should verify your information before condemning me out of hand!"

A stony silence greeted this, Christina aware that she had stumbled on to holy ground.

"I-I'm sorry—"

"There is no need to apologise," he cut her short, turning back to the panoramic view. "The error was mine."

An even stonier silence now clothed the atmosphere as Christina's eyes nervously travelled ceilingwards where buxom nymphs and chubby cherubs bedecked Jupiter with floral garlands in gay abandon—she feeling she ought to say something but not quite sure what.

"How did you meet Cousin Charles?" he fired unexpectedly.

Christina jumped. "W-We met quite by chance, whilst out r-riding—in the w-woods beyond the estate—"

"Beyond the estate?"

"W-We didn't mean to disobey you, my lord," she hurried on. "Rebecca's horse bolted over the border without warning, and your cousin was fortunately on hand to come to her rescue."

"I see; and having once broken bounds I gather you continued doing so?" he flung at her, witheringly. "Did I not state, Miss Wansford, that I would provide you with a suitable husband?"

"With all respect, my lord—suited to your taste, not mine."

"And my cousin?" he countered swiftly. "He appealed to your taste?"

Christina prevaricated, selecting her words with care.

"I-I found him quite civil."

He indulged in a cynical smile. "Are we not two of a kind, Charles and I? Do you not find little to choose betwixt us? . . . Faith! Dear Charles will need to be a trifle more adventurous in the future should he wish to revel in your company."

"Little escapes your notice, my lord," she declared in pique. "How foolish of me to believe you had imposed your latest rule in concern for my safety."

"Safety? From what? From whom? 'S life! If I were to surround the entire house with armed guards 'twould not protect you from the one you truly fear . . . would it?"

Christina gulped, discomfort roaming round inside her. She could feel his eyes boring through her but refused to meet them.

"As my cousin is privileged to share your confidence, may I ask if you found his strain of converstion entertaining?"

"O-On the contrary, I found it r-rather un-unpleas . . . ant. . . ."

"But credible, nonetheless?"

Again, Christina could sense him manoeuvring her into a verbal corner as she found it increasingly difficult to supply non-committal answers to his questions, for nought but the voice of insanity would name him a murderer outright.

"I-I'm not sure. . . ."

"Why? What causes you to doubt, Miss Wansford?" he queried scornfully, half turning to throw her a mocking glance. "You think the accusation false? That I am without blemish?"

She gave no indication of the dread gnawing at her heart as she managed to stare him bravely in the eye, her voice remarkably steady.

"Are you trying to convince me of your innocence or guilt, my lord?"

"As my cousin has already regaled you with my sordid past, I am persuaded you require no further assurance of my guilt," he observed sardonically, his interest taken by a dainty Dresden figure, intentionally or otherwise would be impossible to say. "You like my collection?" he queried blandly as if not bothered either way, indicating the shelves of the alcove, well stocked with china treasures. "Sadly akin to the fair sex, don't you think? Delightful to the eye, but alas, empty and useless."

Christina ignored the gibe, being anxious to maintain his amiable humour.

"As you do not appear to stand very high in your cousin's esteem, Lord Stryde, is it not possible that his word may be somewhat biased?"

"Perchance it may," he agreed, replacing the little swineherd upon the shelf with his companions. "Though I cannot for the life of me perceive why you should think me frantic to be deemed innocent. Even if I were I—"

"I-If you w-were?" she stammered weakly, her last shred of courage evaporating; for if by some strange mischance she had been mistaken concerning the ring and the blazing barn, there was certainly no mistaking this blantant admission of his devious part in his father's death.

"You can't seriously have thought otherwise?" he drawled with a derisive laugh, wending his way slowly towards her. "I—the personification of every vice and corruption known to man? Whom decent people shun in the street and even Society's most hardened rakes discreetly go out of their way to avoid? With tales of whom fathers seek to shock their rebellious sons into mending their ways, and mothers use to frighten the little ones, warning them that the Wicked Stryde will come and carry them off if they don't eat up all their gruel? Come now, let's be honest!" His sarcasm now reached scathing proportions as his ominous black figure towered over her, obliterating the golden sun from the windows. "You tremble, my dear, with fear—for it can scarce be desire—yet you remain. You do not flee the room. Or have your limbs deserted you, and terror, not valour, rivets you to the chair?"

Howbeit, had she wished to flee the room Christina would have been hard pressed for he now leaned over her, his fingers twining like steel bands round her arms before he raised her effortlessly to her feet. She stood rooted to the spot, marvelling how she was able to do so, unable to utter a sound for every ounce of breath in her body was being utilized to keep heart and lungs functioning, as his hands progressed up her arms . . . shoulders . . . graduating to her soft . . . white . . . neck.

"You are exceedingly brave for a female, Christina, but

alas! twice as foolish to linger 'neath my roof ignoring Fate's warning to be gone, before your doom is sealed."

Had she been able to summon strength Christina realised that it was already too late to protest, and so, closed her eyes to await the end—imprecations to heaven for absolution of her sins swirling frenziedly in her brain pending, with bated breath, the pressure of his fingers to increase . . . but it did not. To her stupefied relief he released her of a sudden, almost roughly, and turned abruptly away.

Christina fell dizzily back into the chair, struggling to re-establish her senses, whilst the Marquess stood facing the empty marble fireplace, his shoulders heaving as he fought to control the rage formenting within him.

"You will not inconvenience me for much longer," he stated hoarsely, when passion permitted. "You will be re-united with your father as soon as it can be arranged!"

Her mouth fell ajar in astonishment.

"I-I beg your . . . p-pardon? M-My f-father?" she stammered stupidly, smothering a mad urge to laugh. "H-He is to be released . . . f-from the D-Debtors' . . . P-Prison?"

"And your family residence restored."

"Whitegables!" she gasped, utterly overwhelmed, wondering if she were dreaming it all as she had done every night since her arrival at Barrington Hall. "B-But how? Why? Surely you don't intend settling his debts and buying back our home out of your own fortune?"

"You plan to prevent me?" he parried with a sneer.

"Y-You can't, my lord! It—It runs into thousands!"

" 'Tis a trifling price to pay to have my house the peaceful well-ordered domicile it was prior to your advent. No! I beg you—spare me your gratitude!" he appended with a forbidding gesture as she made to thank him effusively be-

107

fore he should quit the room. "I assure you, my reasons are quite uncomplimentary to yourself, and motivated purely from self-interest . . . simply that it relieves me of the thankless task of finding you a husband, and rids my house of your onerous presence!"

The door closed behind him, and Christina was left debating whether she wanted most of all to scream with delight at the unexpected good tidings, or with frustration at the knowledge that his insults had the power to cut quite deeply, deeper perhaps than he himself realised.

CHAPTER EIGHT

Joy! Pure unadulterated joy now superabounded from Christina's heart as full import of the wonderful news registered in her dazed brain—generated not entirely by the prospect of being reunited with her dear parent, though naturally, this was a prime contributory factor. No, it was not until this moment that she came to appreciate how greatly her chances were enhanced of attaining her heart's burning desire, for as her father would be resuming the responsibilty of her legal guardian, it would prove no difficult task for Christina to cajole him into granting his consent to her marriage with Black Dan. Therefore, all she had to do was wring a proposal from Dan, which she readily admitted might place a little extra strain upon her power of persuasion, but he would no doubt come about in the end. After all, he had already expressed an urgency to leave the perilous county of Hampshire—what difference did it make if he fled to France or Yorkshire? Yes, he could go with her to Whitegables where no one would recognise him, not having even heard of him. And they had enough wealth between them to live, if not in luxury, then in certain comfort for the rest of their days, with some to spare to hire the services of the best physician in the land to set Dan's scarred face to rights. She had heard of wonderful salves from the Orient which could transform the most appallingly disfigured features overnight. Then they could marry and live happily ever after.

During that week further whoops of delight were heard to resound from the two girls upon delivery of new gowns from a London mantua-maker of the highest repute, and the deciding of costumes for Rebecca's betrothal masquerade, which thrilled the younger girl to the point of confessing all particulars of her splendid costume to anyone who cared to devote an ear, and planning a costume for her father before he had even darkened the portals of Barrington Hall. All was indeed revelry and joy, with the great house finally relieved of its mourning favours.

Consequently, it was with an exceedingly light heart that Christina rode out to meet her Dan on the Friday, unable to see how he could possibly cavil at her suggestion to relinquish their present partnership for a lifelong one.

Nevertheless, upon the arrival at their favourite oak she had to own to feeling a trifle saddened by the knowledge that they would no longer meet as Brothers of the Road. Never again ride together through the night and thrill to the cry of 'stand and deliver'—or sit under the stars whilst he regaled her with his tales, terrifying tales, side-splitting funny tales, and utterly fantastic tales which earned him her speechless admiration for his power of inventive genius.

Christina drew herself up with a start as the faint drum of hoofbeats was borne to her ear, racing through the forest, growing louder and louder, her heart drumming in unison until her eardrums pounded with the noise and her horse emitted a shrill whinny in recognition of an old friend. And all at once, there he was—the man whom she realised she not only loved but worshipped like a god.

If she harboured any underlying guilt about not ending the association in accordance with the Marquess's commands it was instantly dispelled as her eyes drank in the intoxicating sight of his tall romantic figure clad in caped surtout, with cocked hat dipped over his eyes and neckerchief streaming on the night breeze, astride his huge black horse—for she than knew she could never give him up, no matter what the price.

As he dismounted she turned away, her head in a spin as she fought frantically to recall the precise wording of her proposition, grave misgivings gnawing at her concerning whether he would now condescend to accept her as his mopsy let alone wed her and approve the rest of her scheme.

Following a civil enquiry into her state of health and if she was quite recovered from her harrowing experience in the fire, he fell silent, obviously possessed of a strange humour as he paced the ground, seemingly eager to be gone. Indeed, it almost appeared as if he had as much weighing on his mind as she, and perhaps wording some kind of announcement of his own, but in which direction? A proposal of marriage—or a declaration of farewell?

The prolonged silence which he seemed loth to break was rapidly becoming unbearable, but Christina did not know how to begin. She longed to flash a glance at him but did not dare, knowing if she once fell victim to the spell of his eyes she would be utterly undone. And so she continued to twist a blade of grass nervously round her forefinger, wishing she had positioned herself more strategically in the shadows, and not in direct line of the moon where her every expression, movement, could be clearly observed, and which she could sense he was taking full advantage of.

"Christina," he said of a sudden—causing chaos in her bosom.

"Y-Yes?" she managed to stammer, though her voice rang peculiar.

"Do you remember what I said when last we met?"

She could remember perfectly well every single word he had ever uttered but elected to delay the issue.

"Y-You mean about m-me being c-cozening?"

"No," he replied flatly, apparently in no mood for pleasantries. "About me fleeing the country."

Of course she remembered! How could she have forgotten when it had burned fiercely in her brain ever since?

"Y-Yes, Dan." The two simple words almost choked her, knowing when next he spoke it would be to pronounce sentence—life with him, or a living death without.

He paused—what seemed an interminable pause—before stating quickly: "I must go sooner than planned—even now the constables are raking the area. . . . I must leave—tonight."

A cry of bitter anguish escaped her. "Oh no, Dan! No!—n-not now?" At this unexpected turn of events caution was thrown to the winds along with her proposal, and she blurted out in one breath: "Oh, Dan, take me with you—please? Please, you must! I-I'll go anywhere . . . suffer anything! I'll be no trouble, I swear! Only please don't leave me—please!"

112

"It's impossible! I cannot imperil your life along with my own—"

"It's already imperilled! I beseech you, Dan! Please take me? I-I'd rather die with you than live without you!"

"You're a sentimental fool!" he snapped irascibly, flinging away from her as if about to go.

"You must take me! You must! I-I can't bear it! ... I love you, Dan! ... I-I've tried not to—I've really tried—but it's no use! I-It's too powerful for me to overcome—"

"There's only one way to overcome it, Christina, and that's to say goodbye. I'm sorry, but in any case, I'm afraid we must."

"No, Dan!" she gasped out, near to panic, "Th-There's another way! W-We can steal away now ... tonight ... to York. I-I'll take you to York ... to my home, White-gables! You'll love it, Dan—truly. I'll hide you there until the danger is past. No one will ever know. Th-There's a priest-hole—"

"York!" he ejaculated in horror, as if she had gone raving mad.

Christina returned a bewildered stare. "D-Don't you like York, Dan? Why? What's wrong with it?"

"York can be a very unhealthy place for members of the High Toby—as one named Turpin would testify were he not prostrate 'neath a tombstone. No, Christina, we must bid our adieux. Don't blame yourself; I am the one at fault. I should have made allowances for your youth and the fact that you are, after all, a woman. I-I hope you will forgive me."

If he had informed her that she was to be hanged on the morrow she could not have been more stricken as those dreaded words fell on her ears. He couldn't mean it. Surely he would reconsider?

113

"No, Dan!—not that!" she appealed frantically, wringing her hands, her bosom heaving tumultuously as she dogged his heels back and forth over the grass. "I-I'll do anything, I swear on all I hold dear! I'll even try my hardest to hate you, I promise. Only please, please! d-don't forsake m-me."

"Christina, it's no use—"

"I can hate quite intensely when I choose. I once had a friend whom I positively abhorred. Y-You wouldn't credit it but I—"

"Christina!" he bellowed, determined to be heard. "Your tears and entreaties will not sway me! We must part our ways! The idea of you tied to me for the rest of your life is unthinkable. You're still a child—you will soon forget."

He made to bypass her but she sank to the ground, hugging his booted feet, refusing to let him go, her passionate pleas punctuated with sobs as tears coursed down her face. With a sigh he stooped to unclasp her fingers, and raising her up tried to console her whilst tenderly drying her eyes on his kerchief.

"You will think me a heartless brute—and rightly so—but someday when you are wed to some rich nobleman I hope you will think kindly of me and perhaps appreciate this good advice I now give you. Christina—are you listening?"

She nodded, dumb with sheer wretchedness, her heart torn asunder.

"Go back to your Barrington Hall. Tuck yourself up in bed with a hot posset. Tomorrow, the world and Black Dan won't seem such a rotten pair after all—you'll see!"—and patting her cheek he clapped hat to head and mounted his horse without further ado.

But before galloping off some strange premonition urged him to glance behind—and what met his gaze turned him ashen.

Christina still stood where he had left her, but with loaded pistol to head like one in a daze. Unleashing a terrible oath he hurled himself from his animal and grabbed her pistol-arm as she fired. There was a shattering explosion and the deadly missile whizzed past his cocked hat at uncomfortably close range, to disappear with a whine into the darkness. Livid with rage, he wrenched the offending weapon out of her grasp and flung it far into the night; then demented, struck her with the full force of his hand across her face, growling through his teeth: "You raving lunatic! What damned good would that do?"

Shocked, dazed, and mute with despair, Christina could only stare at him petrified with grief by the knowledge that she must bear the crucifying burden of her future life without him, while he stared back, confused, bewildered, like a blind man suddenly given his sight, seeing her for the very first time . . . as he gradually awakened to the frightening realisation . . . that his soul was no longer his own. The next instant his hard brutal shell cracked and with an agonising groan he dragged her savagely into his arms and the storm of passion broke to engulf them both in its raging billows, his arms enveloping her tighter and tighter, straining her to him with a desperate, vital yearning which none but she could satisfy, his mouth searching hungrily for hers to devour her in kiss after kiss of vehement desire.

Christina returned his kisses wildly, clinging feverishly to him, not even trying to reason his irrational behaviour or establish if she were awake or dreaming. The emotional tide swept through her like a maelstrom as he took her face in his hands and began to rain fervent kisses on her hair, eyes, face, neck.

"Forgive me! Forgive me, Christina!" he punctuated his impassioned outburst. "I-I don't know what possesses me! . . . I swear, I didn't mean to hurt you . . . but you drive me insane! I've never met a woman like you . . . firing my blood the way you do, the way no woman has ever done before . . . Why? . . . How? . . . I was so sure I wouldn't get involved! . . . so sure you wouldn't drag me over the edge with your captivating beauty and witchery . . . yet, here I am, floundering . . . drowning in a sea of uncontrollable desire . . . wondering how to survive, but at the same time . . . not quite certain . . . that I . . . want to. . . ."

Again his lips found hers to weld them together in a renewed burst of passion, drawing the very breath from her body to replace it with something even more vital to her existence.

"I love you, Christina! How can I deny it! I love you with all my heart, and want you desperately! . . . I ache and crave for you night and day . . . I've battled madly to ignore it but it's no use . . . you mean more to me than anyone—anything . . . more than my very life . . . but I cannot insult you with an offer of marriage. You are far, far, beyond my reach—"

"No, Dan! No!" she cried out wildly. "You mustn't talk so! It isn't like you to admit defeat. No one is beyond anyone's reach. We are all equal in the sight of God."

He firmly put her from him. "You? I? Your guardian? We're all equal?"

"To me you are just as noble as he, Dan. I don't love

116

you any less because you are what you are. Can't you understand that you are the only man I want and ever shall?"

"You forget, Christina, that I am no ordinary man, and you are no ordinary woman. My soul is as black as hell and yours—pure and unblemished. It would be like Satan wedding a Vestal Virgin!"

"But if we love each other—"

"You aren't enacting a drama! Believe me, I am deeply honoured that your love for me is so overwhelming that it blinds you to reality. For example, have you ever stopped to think that love alone may not be enough?" he questioned, eyeing her strangely as she stood contorting her hat into a variety of shapes. "There is much about me you do not know, and may not like. . . . You might think me cowardly, deceitful—even hate me."

"Never, Dan! Never!" she screamed aghast, running up to throw her arms round him in reassurance. "I could never hate you no matter how hard I tried! What a preposterous thing to say!"

"All the same," he responded impatiently, guiding her across to her horse and helping her into the saddle, suddenly anxious to have her leave. "I shall delay my departure for one month—"

"But the law. Your life is in deadly peril!"

"Fear not, I have an excellent refuge. Meanwhile, you must ponder the matter well. . . . If, by the appointed hour you are of the same heart and mind, then meet me. I shall come undisguised that you may see clearly the man you would give yourself to, and shall confess my past— though it does not make very pleasant listening." He paused, as if selecting his words with meticulous care.

"Should your love—by some miracle—survive all this, then I shall ask you to be my wife—"

"But why must I wait, Dan!" broke in Christina, loth to endure yet another month of suspense, fretting about her indeterminate future—not that she believed his looks or whatever he chose to confess would bring about any dramatic change in her feelings, for no matter what he had done or looked like she would still want to wed him—she was adamantly sure. "Why can't you unmask now?"

"No!" he cried out, in what sounded to Christina very akin to alarm—even dread—which leapt like a flame to ignite her inherent curiosity. Granted, she had experienced her moments of frenzied desire to see his face and the extent of the scars, but as he exploded like a cannon whenever she as much as hinted at it, and there seemed little chance of them ever aspiring to wedlock, she had deemed it politic not to pursue her selfish interest any further. But this occasion was rather different. This time, Dan himself had made the suggestion, which he had never done before, and although the note of alarm in his voice would seem to imply that he was yet averse to unmasking, the very fact that he had proposed it seemed to suggest otherwise.

Having uttered his protest he took a quick step back in retreat, raising a restraining hand to the mysterious black material of an unusual depth, concealing his face from hairline to upper lip, but not quick enough as Christina tore the mask from his face—to blench in horror at the dreadful disfigurement which met her eyes—more abhorrent than anything she could have imagined—glowing, ghoulish in the moonlight like something supernatural— before he hastily concealed it from view with a muttered oath—features distorted and mocking, with the nose disjointed and the eyes swollen and discoloured in gruesome shades of green and blue—like the grotesque clowns she had seen as a child at Tadcaster Fair, with their huge hideous faces to terrify her—but nothing compared to the terror and revulsion she experienced just then.

In a fit of madness she stabbed viciously at the mare's flanks with her heels, and emitting a whinny of pain the poor animal sprang into action.

"Christina! . . . c-come back . . . !"—it was a cry of searing agony from the heart—but she did not glance back as she charged off along the road, screaming and sobbing wildly until she finally reached Barrington Hall, exhausted and trembling as with ague, and, staggering up the stairs to her bedchamber, Chistina collapsed in her closet, and was violently sick.

CHAPTER NINE

It was three full days before Christina managed to quit her bed and should not have done so even then but for the rumour circulating among the servants that a physician was to be sent for to diagnose the precise nature of her indisposition.

Once up and dressed she wandered aimlessly about, heeding nothing or no one like a clockwork doll, until her senses gradually reawakened and feeling crept back into her being, when she was able to delve into her inmost heart and question her emotions—resulting in frequent bouts of tears interspersed with fits of moribund depression. Thus, she spent the days, but the nights were worst of all, during which she was buffeted unmercifully in tempestuous seas of weird apparitions when she would wake screaming, bathed in perspiration at the recurring vision of those horrifying features, convinced she could never look on them again and retain her sanity. But come the morning and she was consumed with the most heart-rending compassion for him, mortified with shame at her hostile reaction and bitter betrayal.

After days and nights of strenuous emotional battles, the days finally proved the victors, for Christina could never forget the wonderful experiences she and Dan had shared, together with their profound love, all of which was too, too precious to be lightly cast aside. Now, she was determined to keep the appointment when the month expired, hoping, though he should deem the arrangement now void under the terrible circumstances, there was a slender chance that he might still come—but once again she overlooked the powerful intervention of Fate.

It chanced one afternoon as she sat in the well-stocked library of Barrington Hall, browsing through volume upon volume in the faint hope of finding something to distract her mind, that Rebecca burst in upon her in a fury of indignation, slamming the door to relieve her feelings, and storming across to where her sister sat poised with a copy of Shakespeare's sonnets in her hand.

"What is it this time, Becky?" she sighed, replacing the morocco-bound book on the shelf, hoping in vain that she was not going to be called upon at such a time to wrestle with another of her young sister's tantrums.

"He had no right, Chris!" screamed Rebecca in vexation, stamping her dainty foot on the sumptuous rug which responded with a dull unimpressive thud. "No right whatsoever! I am at perfect liberty to—"

"Do calm yourself, Becky. Who had no right to do what?" she asked impatiently, wishing Rebecca would gain control of herself and enable her to get the gist of the grievance.

"Lord Stryde!" she exploded, wondering how Christina could possibly think 'he' meant anyone else, for her dearest Anthony would never provoke her so. "Snatched the *Gazette* from under my very nose, if you please, while I was actually reading it—and without so much as a by your leave!"

Christina shrugged helplessly. It was typical of the Marquess to act thus. Surely Rebecca was used to it by now?

"Perhaps he wanted to read it himself," she suggested not too helpfully. "Though he might have requested it politely."

"Of course he didn't want to read it!" snapped Becky scornfully. "It was over a week old! Besides, why should he lock it away in his desk drawer and order me not to mention a word of it to you?"

This aroused a modicum of Christina's interest. "Are you sure, Becky?"

"Absolutely sure! I was scanning the Society Column for notice of my forthcoming engagement, when he suddenly seized it for no reason that I could see."

"But what was that about me not being told? Did he say why?"

"No," returned Rebecca, blankly. "Except that it would avoid a deal of trouble and embarrassment—that is, after questioning me for a full fifteen minutes to make sure you had not already seen it?"

"Seen what?" queried Christina, curiosity and confusion waxing amain.

"The *Gazette*, you ninny-hammer!" answered her irate sister.

"I mean what exactly in the *Gazette*? It must have been something vastly important."

Rebecca's comely face fell downcast, as she threw her

sister a sheepish look and fiddled with the ribbons adorning her rose-pink gown.

"Don't tell me you had your nose in nothing but the Society Column?" went on Christina, exasperated.

"Well, wouldn't you, if you were about to become affianced?" Becky retaliated, piqued. "Apart from which, I wasn't given much time to see anything else, even if I'd wanted to."

"You must remember something?"

Rebecca shook her fair curls forlornly.

"Then perhaps you can remember what the Marquess did with it?" pursued Christina, rapidly becoming convinced that the newspaper held some vital link with her guardian and his deceased father, he being so obviously anxious for her and Becky not to see it.

"I've already told you," cried Becky irritably. "He locked it away in his desk, in the study, to make sure I couldn't get it. I watched slyly from the door of the Blue Drawing Room and saw him enter. Then I heard the drawers of his desk open and close and the jingle of keys—not long after which he came out again."

"You are sure he didn't burn it?"

"Oh, no, I'm certain of that! Anyway, he didn't have time, there being no fire in the grate."

"Good," approved Christina.

"W-Why good, Chris?" questioned Becky, puzzled. "What d'you mean?"

Christina was saved the trouble of having to respond to this by the opportune entrance of a footman who bore a dish of sweetmeats, including sugar-plums and marchpane mice—to Rebecca's delight and her sister's relief, and before the first mouse was decapitated the entire incident was completely forgotten—forgotten by the younger Miss

Wansford perhaps, but not the elder, the cogs of whose imaginative genius were already well in circulation.

After supper that evening Christina experienced some difficulty in suppressing her excitement at thoughts of what she had planned, for she was more determined than ever to lay hands on the mysterious *Gazette* and nurtured every intention of doing so when the household was asleep in a few hours. Rebecca should have preferred to amuse herself upon the harpsichord writhing in the death-throes of vocal homage to the God of Love, but instead, agreed to help her sister pass the time with a card game, unable to understand why she should be so on tenterhooks. And so the two indulged in a game of patience, but perhaps impatience would have been more aptly suited to Christina.

The hours finally dragged by and the two climbed the stairs to their respective rooms, Rebecca retiring to her bed to sleep whilst Christina lay still fully clothed upon hers, cherishing her plan to raid the study. She lay for an appreciable time until she heard the grandfather clock in the Marble Hall toll out the hour of one, when all was dark and deathly silent and so admirably suited to her need. Dare she venture forth now?

Feverish curiosity beckoned her from the bed, and pausing only to take up a small bundle of implements and a candle which she had set ready to one side, she crept off down to the study.

Once inside the room, she hastened over to the desk and set down her bundle to light the candle. This done, she then made a cursory examination of all six drawers, discovering the two smallest firmly locked. Undoubtedly the *Gazette* she sought was inside one of these but she searched quickly through the others first to find, as expected, nothing but a heap of uninteresting papers and documents, and so she turned her attention back to the locked drawers.

To her annoyance, none of her collection of oddly shaped keys from bygone caskets fitted the even more oddly shaped locks, therefore, taking up a knife (appropriated from the supper-table) she set to work. After prodigious grunting and heaving, the first of the two drawers burst open, and following a thorough turn-out Christina discovered bundles of bonds, receipts and banknotes, still more papers—and a small but deadly-looking pistol. On impulse she slammed the drawer, to immediately regret it and hold her breath, listening, hoping no one had heard. Satisfied that all was well, she proceeded to the final drawer, now wishing she had searched it first and thus saved time.

Again she wrenched and struggled to force the lock which proved even more stubborn than the other, snapping the knife clean in half and bending and twisting her scissors, hairpins and guardian's paper-knife out of all recognition. But with a particularly vigorous tug the offending drawer finally flew open and there, to her delight, lay the treasured *Gazette*.

Snatching it up, she spread it out with care on the desk and drew the candle closer to peruse the contents the better, turning each page as if it were some sacred ancient manuscript: but to her bitter disappointment not a single word printed therein bore any reference to her guardian at all, let alone his deceased sire. Once again did she scrutinise the newspaper, page by page—a little less impetuously, paying more attention to the detailed smaller print, until she reached the page directly opposite the Society Column.

This, she was about to flick over like the rest with a grunt of vexation when her eye was arrested by two small paragraphs in the bottom right-hand corner. Why, she could not at first say, as they seemed to bear little significance to her present attitude of mind, until a certain familiar name, stressed in bold black characters, leapt up from the page of a sudden to send a searing pang of horror shivering through her body, turning her very blood to ice.

Helplessly drawn by a strange sensation of terror and foreboding, her eyes devoured these shattering words:

> *'It will be of great Cheer to all upright, honest Citizens to know that one, Black Dan, Highwayman, and notorious Terror of the Hampshire Highways, was apprehended Tuesday last, and is now safely under Lock and Key in Newgate Prison, awaiting Trial.'*

It then went on to give a detailed account of how, when and where the arrest took place but the words swam before her eyes, making it impossible for her to continue. She stood petrified, numb with shock, as if her whole body had ceased to function, until she choked on a sob and fell grief-stricken into a chair.

With this disastrous news came the solution to her heart problem. She was his body and soul. Despite his disfigurement she loved him and could not face the future without him, though it meant a life of martyrdom. Christina groaned as she recalled his last agonised cry as she had spurned him and ridden away, the soul-tortured cry of a doomed man, which she had deliberately ignored.

Eventually overcoming her grief she stood erect. So,

Dan was to be the Marquess's next victim. These were the dire consequences he could not be answerable for if she dared to disobey him. In no time at all, Christina had worked herself up into an inferno of wrath against her guardian, firm in the conviction that his hand, and none other, had placed the noose about Dan's neck.

Alas! It was at this crucial moment that the object of her antipathy chose to appear, as a soft but very distinct 'click' was heard over by the door, which instantly drew her attention. With a strangled gasp she realised before she raised the candle to illuminate the face, that the tall sinister figure draped in the purple robe of quilted brocade was the Marquess.

Whose rage was the greater would be impossible to say as they stood rigid, their eyes cauterising each other, like a panther and tigress suddenly coming face to face in the blackest jungle—until Christina thudded down the candlestick and grabbed the twisted paper-knife—to attack or defend, whichever chanced, evidently of the opinion that the reason for her anger far outweighed the appalling act of ransacking his desk.

Not until the Marquess had his fury well under control did he make any attempt to speak.

"I trust your curiosity is amply satisfied?" he queried with difficulty, advancing across the expanse of thick Turkish carpet to the wine-cabinet to select himself a drink strong enough for the occasion, while Christina stood fanning the flames of her anger, unable to see what more she had to lose by giving full licence to, for if Dan was to die what would life be worth?

"Is this how the Marquess of Stryde ensures implicit obedience to his commands?" she cried wildly, slamming her hand down on the *Gazette*. "Is this how you could be so certain I'd never see him again?"

The Marquess held his peace as he filled a second glass and approached her to offer it.

"Would you accept my word, if I were to swear on oath that I had nothing whatever to do with it?"

"No!" she sobbed frantically, dashing the glass clean from his hand to send it crashing into the corner, splashing the costly furnishings with the contents.

For one explosive moment Christina quaked in her slippers for it certainly seemed that he would throttle her—or that she would at least follow the wine-glass—and she backed instinctively until she felt the cold hard window against her back.

Again Lord Stryde managed to restrain himself, but turned away lest she provoke him beyond endurance.

"The only thing I am prepared to admit is that I owe you a deal of explaining; and as it is obviously futile attempting to do so at the moment, I shall instead, suggest you take yourself back to your bed—"

"Bed!" she echoed, as if it were the most preposterous suggestion imaginable at two in the morning. "If I take myself anywhere, my Lord Marquess, it will be to London!"

"I assure you, Miss Defiance, London is out of the question—if I have to chain you to the bedpost to prove it!"

At present the term 'defiance' suited her to perfection as she stood seething by the window, wringing the paper-knife in her hands as if anxious to put it to use—but not for the purpose originally designed.

"You do not seem to appreciate the fact, sir, that the man I love is locked away condemned to die," she snapped. "How can you therefore expect me to go calmly back to bed to rest content in the knowledge that he may be about to mount the scaffold at dawn this very morning?"

"In which case, there would be little you could do to save him even if you left immediately and galloped all the way non-stop," he pointed out with infuriating common sense.

"I see your game," she cried incensed, "typical of your cunning, Lord Stryde! To have the man I love arrested and your competition descreetly eliminated so that you can have me to yourself to seduce at your pleasure. Is there no end to your wickedness?"

"By the death! 'Twould seem your mind is even more infernal than mine. You do me grave injustice. There is much you do not understand and I cannot bring myself to burden you further.... You have sustained a terrible blow this night, and I would not add to it by confessing—"

"Spare me your confessions, sir! What you have done is betwixt you and your Maker. Surely you do not mean to humiliate me the more by begging my forgiveness for your heinous deed?" She flung the paper-knife back on to the desk and swung round to face the window, indignation personified. "La! It would be almost as absurd as my begging you to use your influence to secure his release."

"Release!" he echoed contemptuously. "Releasing your jailbirds is rapidly becoming a habit!"

"Yes! Release him and thus prove you truly had no part in it!" she rounded on him, ignoring the gibe.

"My dear girl, I tried to spare you this, but now that you have seen and read all I view it as a blessing in disguise. Indeed, 'tis the best thing that could have

129

chanced—forcing you to see the folly of your ways, give up this rogue and forget he ever existed."

Christina's eyes flared with passion. "Never! I shall never give him up without a desperate fight to save him! Be reasonable, Lord Stryde. I can't let him die! I can't! I-I love him . . . and m-must make . . . every . . . effort. . . ."

Her voice trailed away as she realised he was no longer listening, no longer interested in her arguments. For or against was all one and the same to him at present as he slowly traversed the room, his brow creased in thought.

He came to a halt immediately in front of her, so close that she could feel the soft brocade of his robe brushing against her arm as he stood looking down on her, gnawing his lip as if in some quandary, his handsome face deeply troubled and framed by his thick black hair, which loosely draped his shoulders.

As he stood thus towering over her in the flickering candlelight Christina, for the first time, began to marvel at the serenity of the night and how infinitely peaceful everything was, aware that so much had happened in the past hour that she had not had time to notice it, though even more astonished that she should notice it at all with so much at stake. But gradually—ashamed as she would have been to own it—her terrible grief over Dan and her problem of rescuing him seemed to fade into the distance as if not now of prime importance, and something else in its stead was creeping over her—a weak trembling feeling capable of quickening heartbeat and breathing, and banishing all else from her mind—a kind of enchantment, as she gazed up into those dark fathomless eyes, to read in their hidden depths a message she had never read there before and which almost frightened her . . . yet not quite.

To her further surprise she found herself warming to him, her heart actually going out to him in sympathy, but for what exactly, she could not tell. It was as if he were drawing everything emotionally from her with the pain in those soul-stirring eyes—everything, moreover, that she was suddenly only too willing to give to alleviate the dire suffering he seemed to be undergoing, of which he made her feel the direct cause.

But she was not alone in her unusual experience, for Lord Stryde's manner had changed too. He was no longer the self-assured callous being she had always deemed him, and when he ventured to speak his voice was the gentlest whisper.

"Christina . . . I-I find myself in some dilemma . . . there is something I would ask . . : something I must know, though you may think it strange . . . and unfeeling. . . ."

"I-I understand," she murmured, swimming in a becalmed sea of emotion.

He remained tense, not daring to breathe lest he break the spell before she had told him what he needed desperately to know.

"I cannot go on until I know . . . if . . . if. . . ."

"Yes?"

He struggled inwardly, having great difficulty putting into words the emotional enigma devouring him.

". . . if you had never met this man . . . would you . . . could you have possibly c-cared . . . for . . . me?"

"I-In what way, my lord?" stammered Christina, conscious of his warm breath on her cheek.

The Marquess closed his eyes and muttered a curse, his forehead moist with perspiration, then tried again.

"Could you have cared for me in the way you care for him?"

Christina stared at him harder, beginning to appreciate the significance of his words, oblivious to how bewitching she looked with lips slightly parted, her skin glowing like translucent ivory in the dim light, remains of the tears glistening on her long lashes, while her rich chestnut hair cascaded down over the voluptuousness of her half-exposed bosom.

"Y-You mean . . . c-could I have . . . loved you?"

The Marquess winced at the word, and the spell was shattered.

Christina blinked her eyes as if waking from a deep sleep, to regard him anew, seeing him in a different aspect, and her voice had not only lost its warmth but was quite frigid.

"Am I permitted to enquire, my lord, if you could have loved me in return?"

"I could have . . . c-cared for you—yes."

His evasion of the crucial word was conspicuous in the extreme.

"But not loved?" she pressed him unmercifully.

"Yes!" he shouted with impatience.

"When you cannot bear even the sound of the word?" she parried, misinterpreting the implication behind his question, though more furious with herself for momentarily forgetting her imperative mission in saving Dan from the gallows. "Indeed why, sir? So that you may add my name to your long list of conquests?"

The Marquess flinched as her arrow hit its mark, and turned away, striving to recover his equilibrium, one elegant hand adhered to his burning forehead. When he eventually removed it his face was the impassive mask he affected for the world at large, his eyes cold and merciless.

"What a question to ask!" she went on, her bosom swelling with indignation. "When my heart lies mangled at your feet over another. One whom you have deliberately sought to destroy though he did you no harm—and one whom I shall never forget. You might as lief ask me to forget that I was ever born."

"All very admirable, but not very sensible!" he flung back. " 'Tis high time you gave some thought to your future and the impressive array of eligible bachelors who will be attending your sister's masquerade next week—"

"I shall never marry anyone but Dan! And if I never see him again he will take my heart with him always—to the very grave."

"Don't be a lovelorn idiot," he rasped caustically. "You evidently do not appreciate it, but I am offering you a lucrative way out of your predicament which you would do well to consider."

"I have no need of your charitable offers," she cast at him tartly. "The love we bear each other cannot be measured in wealth and position. It is far beyond earthly desires; but I'd be better served saving my breath to cool my pottage than wasting it trying to plead love's cause to one who knows not the meaning of the word!"

The glass Lord Stryde held suddenly surrendered to the pressure of his grasp as he wrestled with his self-discipline, and splintered, cutting deep into his fingers. Nevertheless, when he spoke his voice was quite steady.

"You think I know nought of love—and its constant companions anguish and despair—which you must suffer now and in the years to come?"

"Why? Why must I suffer?" she besought him, growing distraught. "Why won't you just let me go—"

"I am saving you a wasted journey."

Fear gripped her heart. "Wh-What do you mean?"

The Marquess replenished his glass with brandy for the third time. "Even now it is too late . . . he is already gone."

Christina gave a cry of horror, pivoting her head from side to side in denial, unable to accept it, refusing to accept it—mouthing soundless incoherencies.

"No! No!" she gasped finally. "I-It's impossible! You lie! It merely states in the *Gazette* that he was apprehended and sent to prison—"

"And did you look at the date?"

She seized the paper to tear frantically at the sheets in search for . . . November eighth! The *Gazette* was almost three weeks old!

"But he could still be alive!" she rounded on him anew, refusing to relinquish the battle. "His execution may have been delayed—"

"You are clutching at straws!"

"Well, he may have escaped—or been granted a last-minute reprieve—"

"Or a Crown Pardon?"

"Oh, Lord Stryde!" she now begged with the same fervour that she had reviled him a moment age, completely forgetting to whom she was appealing in her distress. "We must leave at once! We must ride to London—"

"We?" he queried with disdain, prising her fingers from his brocade-clad arm.

"You must help me! You must! I-I have no one else to turn to and I cannot go alone."

"You forget Cousin Charles. Is not he more worthy of your trust?"

"But he does not have your position and influence."

"No! And it would avail you nought if he did for you will never escape me!" he snarled vindictively, relishing her squirming and suffering. "This time there is no haggling nor promises! This time your highwayman is gone—for good!"

"No!" she shrieked. "You can't let him die! You can't!"

"He is already dead!" he thundered, but to no purpose for she kept on and on, beseeching him as never before, in desperation for the life of the man she loved.

But, though her anguished appeal would have racked many a human heart, his remained obdurate, adamantly refusing to listen as she crumbled before him, her emotions running rampant, but she made no effort to restrain them, there being no point any more.

"Why? Why?" she burst out anew, her spirit broken. "Why must you hate me so? What harm have I done you? How do I merit such punishment by merely falling in love?"

Lord Stryde made no response, keeping his eyes averted from the wretched misery manifest on her face as he mixed a concoction in a glass, then held it to her lips, commanding her to drink, brooking no refusal when she made to protest before she surrendered weakly and drank it down to the last drop.

"You will now retire to your chamber and obliterate the grievous past from your mind completely," he informed her conclusively. "That potion will help you—"

"Why, wh-what was it?" she stammered with misgiving, beginning to suffer the first peculiar effects. "You plan to

135

obliterate me as well as my mind . . . y-you've poisoned me . . . I-I'm d-dying—"

"You are no such thing! It was a simple drug to make you sleep—"

"For ever!" she persisted hysterically. "It was poison! I-I've been poisoned! I feel it . . . over . . . coming m-me. . . . I'm so t-tired . . . so . . . w-weak. . . ."

And with this final accusation on her lips, she sank into his arms in a profound sleep, leaving the Marquess to bear her recumbent form upstairs to her bedchamber.

CHAPTER TEN

It was late the following afternoon when Christina began to stir from her comatose sleep, struggling to disentangle fact from fantasy—fact being what had actually occurred prior to her descent into the lap of Morpheus, and fantasy, the weird dreams which had disturbed her sleep, of the Marquess, his Cousin Charles, Molly Anders, Dan and herself, all dancing around Tyburn Tree singing the *Ring o' Roses*—unable to understand why Mr Liddell and her maid should be included in the party. And another of Molly executing a dance macabre round her bed, bending over her, crowing and cackling like a witch that she was going to become the Marchioness of Stryde!

Christina next wondered if she were alive or dead, recalling the revolting white liquid the Marquess had forced down her throat whilst laying violent hands upon her. And Dan? Was he dead too ... or perhaps mounting the scaffold at that very moment? Was there yet time to save him? Wylton Weir! She must get to Wylton Weir at all cost, and enlist the aid of Charles Liddell, who would not hesitate to help her. She would indite a message and despatch it with Molly, immediately—or as soon as she could raise her eyelids, which seemed to be weighted down.

Where was she—in heaven? Everything was very quiet and a blazing light shone across her eyes—but she could hear something quite close at hand . . . breathing! Spasmodic breathing!—of what?

Compelling her eyelids apart despite the blinding sun from the window, she turned her head towards the sound, blinking rapidly to discern a human form—masculine— who was taking her hand gently in his and murmuring in concern but she could not distinguish whom until her sight finally returned and she recognised the features.

"F-Father!" she gasped, bobbing up with a start—to be sharply brought to account by her head which, for some peculiar reason, felt six times its normal weight and size.

"Take care, child," he cautioned, placing an arm about her shoulders, his gaunt face creased in anxiety as he handed her a glass of restorative. "Here, drink this. It will set you to rights in a trice."

"Wh-What is it?" she queried, swirling the yellow fluid round in the glass, alternately eyeing it and her father with suspicion.

"A little something the Marquess suggested would make you feel better—"

"The Marquess!" she exclaimed, swiftly handing back back the potion. "Kindly inform him that I'd rather suffer my headache."

"Christina! Be reasonable! His lor—"

"I am being reasonable, father—perfectly reasonable! Lord Stryde cannot guarantee me a long life, I admit, but

138

if I were to drink that he might guarantee me a short one!"

Her father gaped incredulously at her. "Ch-Child, you are g-gravely ill! I-I shall summon his lordship's physician at once!"

"Father, I am perfectly sane! As the Marquess has attempted to cut short my life on two occasions already, I am taking stringent precautions against a third."

Sir William was nurturing grievous doubts about his daughter's mental welfare, wondering if the death of his old friend the fourth Marquess and the house of mourning had reacted adversely upon her constitution.

"Y-You jest perhaps, Christina?" he questioned hopefully.

"No, father, I do not jest."

"But there must be some misunderstanding? Wh-What on earth has been happening during my absence? What *do* you mean?"

"It surprises me that you—" Christina stopped short, aware that she was convincing her father of only one thing—that she was quite, quite mad! After all, how could she expect him to be acquainted with the relevant facts? And so she hastily substituted another topic, of more immediate concern. "Oh, do forgive me, father dear!" she gushed, hugging him as best she could from the bed. "You must tell me how you do! Indeed, you look exceedingly well! And just look at your fine new suit!" went on she in genuine approval, experiencing no difficulty in perceiving who had financed his clothes.

Sir William was appreciably puzzled by his daughter's sudden change of manner, but even so dubiously took the bait, despatching her hallucinations from his mind as nothing more serious than some dream she had had; and

139

the subsequent hour was expended in an exchange betwixt father and daughter about all they had undergone during the past year, each discreetly omitting passages from their lives which would give the other the smallest degree of pain, and Sir William ending by stating how greatly he had enjoyed his short stay at the Marquess's castle in Warwickshire, where he had been during the two weeks since his release, and which had unfortunately delayed his reunion with his beloved daughters.

Indeed, it did not take Christina long to appreciate the ethereal heights to which her father esteemed Lord Stryde and just how helplessly he already was 'neath his Machiavellian influence. This being so, she carefully circumvented anything of an inflammatory nature and strove to support her father's high opinion of the Marquess, though it tried her, sorely.

Had Christina elected openly to divulge the true contents of her mind just then, however, her father would not have suffered a moment's hesitation in having her committed to Bedlam, for as he spoke her resources were at work plotting how she was to send Molly to Wylton Weir without the Marquess finding out.

A further hour expired before her father finally took his leave, and barely had the door closed on him than she was out of bed rallying herself together. Staggering across to call her maid she had one thought drumming in her fevered brain—to get to London!

Howbeit, it would appear that the Marquess was still as determined that she should not, for on turning the knob she found, to her extreme annoyance, the door firmly locked! Had this been done by her father who had just quitted the room? If so, it was logical to suppose that he was forewarned of her expected flight—but had he also been told the reason?

The window was her next inspiration. She would knot the bedclothes together and lower herself to the ground as she had heard tell of eloping couples doing. But on peering out of the window to view the thirty-foot drop, a cry of dismay escaped her to see not only one, but two lackeys standing guard immediately below. Evidently Lord Stryde was prepared for all eventualities.

But the more Christina found herself thwarted by the Marquess the more determined she became to evade his clutches, and her next move was to go back to knock loudly on the door, calling out for Molly to come and attend her. At first she thought her summons had passed unheard and was about to rain heavier blows upon the offending door with a shoe, when she detected a thudding footfall, and jingle of keys which rattled in the lock before the door swung open to reveal—not the familiar Molly—but a stout ogre of a woman who, with forbidding look fixed upon even more forbidding visage, informed her in no uncertain manner that her maid had been dismissed that very morning, and until she was replaced with someone more suitable, she (the ogress) would attend her needs. And, locking the door again, promptly betook herself off to bespeak some repast for her charge.

This was taking the matter to extreme! fumed Christina, sinking on to the bed, even more dumbfounded than about the flunkeys on sentry-duty down below. But to dismiss Molly Anders, in whom she had confided since her arrival at Barrington Hall, was the ultimate.

No one was allowed to attend her but Mistress Proudfoot, whom she was rather reluctant to gainsay— had she been in any positon to—and each time she asked to see Rebecca or her father she was politely informed that they were otherwise engaged. Under such rigid conditions Christina soon realised that her escape would need to be postponed until the masquerade when the Marquess would have little alternative but to release her to attend the celebration of her own sister's betrothal, and where (as it now seemed highly unlikely that she would succeed in contacting Mr Liddell) there would be ample opportunity and persons of high standing only too willing to be of service. Thus decided, she bided her time for the remaining few days, struggling to conceal her impatience to be gone and anxiety for Dan's life—praying fervently in her heart that she would arrive in time to save it.

True enough, as she had foreseen she was given leave to attend the ball, and with the aid of three maids carried out her toilette, under the stringent eye of Mistress Proudfoot who tut-tutted in disapproval at her charge's gown for the occasion, the way it clung so immodestly to her form, whether she were supposed to be Queen Guinevere or not.

But though it was her sister's ball and Rebecca was naturally to take pride of place, Christina herself had never looked more ravishing than she did just then as she stood poised before her looking-glass (despite adverse noises issuing from her overseer) her toilette complete. She was draped from top to toe in a white silk gown rather like a robe, trimmed with silver braid which was also skilfully entwined in her rich dark hair. Indeed, their guardian had for once been most generous in placing a handsome sum at their disposal in honour of the event— no doubt to impress Society.

When she was finally permitted to descend the stairs, though under escort of no less a person than her father who was fancifully garbed as a corsair, Christina found that the distinguished guests had already begun to arrive in an odd assortment of guises, bowing and curtsying to Rebecca, a blushing demure Juliet, also in white, and Anthony Wilde, a very fetching Romeo, whose privilege it was to welcome all and sundry, some felicitating the happy couple a trifle prematurely as the official engagement was not to take place until the unmasking at midnight.

Upon entering the Crystal Ballroom she gasped with awe at the breathtaking decoration. Lord Stryde had certainly spared no expense on this important day in her sister's life, though perhaps done more on Mr Wilde's behalf, thought she uncharitably.

The decoration had been the complete responsibility of a certain Monsieur Chevillet (brought especially from Paris) who, with his team of experts, specialised in 'The Grand Occasion' and who in this instance appeared to have excelled himself. The theme was The Garden of Eden, the entire ballroom being transformed into a veritable paradise with potted shrubs and flowers of every hue, also ornamental trees to add an authentic touch, the focal point being the Tree of Knowledge standing impressively in the centre with real fruit suspended from its branches. On either side, illuminated fountains played into great silver bowls wherein swam several varieties of tiny fish, whilst the cascading water reflected the iridescent colours of the lanterns strung across the ceiling—to represent a star-spangled sky. The Marquess's personal musicians up in the musicians' gallery were so obscured by flowers that they could be traced only by the strains of Vivaldi emanating therefrom.

At last Mr Wilde led Rebecca out on to the floor and

the ball commenced, Christina obliged to partner a nephew of the Marquess, Mr Andrew Sinclair, whose stinted conversation she found excessively irritating in her present humour, and alas, who danced little better, spending more time dancing upon her besandalled feet than upon the floor.

Throughout the evening, not once did Christina lose sight of her goal, being constantly on the alert for some trustworthy gentleman of consequence who would be willing to assist in the furtherance of her ambition. But the task was more difficult than she could have forseen, for some were burdened with clucking domineering wives, whilst others would have been indiscreet, disinterested, or downright shocked. And whereas a small proportion would have been only too eager to oblige, it was obvious by their leering and ogling that what they had in mind was the furtherance of their own interests and not hers.

It was some while later that she found herself seated by the side of the ballroom with a certain Sir Nigel Grimshaw and his party, viewing the scene with an air of dejection whilst listening with half an ear to the game being played by the rest of her companions, namely, to establish the identity of the masked guests as they danced by, at intervals, challenging her to compete with them.

"Stake me life on't, ye can't name the pink fairy dancing with Merlin!" exclaimed someone from the rear.

"Miss Jennifer Finley, of course," obliged Christina, forcing an interest.

"Ah! But what of yonder knight, Miss Wansford?" quoth a certain Lord Wilkin in her ear. "What d'you make of him?"

"Aye!" piped up several in support. "Who is St George?"

Christina transferred her gaze across the room to where, sure enough, a tall knight, the top portion only of his body encased in armour—no doubt to facilitate dancing—stood hovering slyly behind some of the guests as though anxious not to be seen in spite of his size. And when the whole group promptly stared across at him, he took fright and disappeared altogether.

"Probably Alexander Willoughby," suggested someone helpfully. "He's quite big."

"No, not Willoughby!" came the chorus of contradiction.

"Yonder harlequin is Willoughby," remarked Sir Nigel. "I recognise his flapping ears."

A gale of laughter went up.

"Ten guineas on Peregrine Philpott!" proposed someone else, but no one seemed inclined to take up the wager.

"A mysterious fellow, Sir Knight," went on Lord Wilkin thoughtfully. "Appeared vastly taken with our Miss Wansford—I'd been observing him for some time. . . ."

"Egad! Ogling our Guinevere was he?" cried Sir Nigel, preparing to do mock battle. "Where is the scoundrel? I'll run him through!"

"Couldn't swear to it, o' course," confessed Lord Wilkin hurriedly. "All that confounded armour, you know. Fellow could ha' been gazing anywhere, I s'pose."

With that, the knight was forgotten by all—except Christina who was now drawn irresistibly to the intriguing St George, and wondering if he would in truth prove to be her champion, refused to be drawn back into the game until Lord Wilkin cried out of a sudden.

"Ha! There's one you won't identify quite so easily, m'

dear—the bewitching senora partnering your guardian."

Despite the fact that she hated the Marquess most intensely, Christina suffered a pang as she followed Lord Wilkin's indication to where a dazzling figure in gold representing the Sun God, Apollo—and exceedingly like the Marquess—was indeed stepping gracefully in time to the music with a dark dangerously attractive female, adorned in a black lace mantilla which hung provocatively over her naked shoulders on to her daringly exposed bosom, while her sensuous body was clad in a red satin gown, ablaze with frills and flounces from hips to hem as affected by the Spanish women. Moreover, she had apparently succeeded in dispelling his ill-humour for he was favouring her with a whimsical smile in response to her amusing comments.

Seemingly he was not on open hostilities with all her sex, seethed Christina inwardly, noting the way his eyes never once left the senora's face.

"Ah!" cried Lord Wilkin. "Name the Roman Centurion with—"

"This childish game grows vastly tedious!" burst forth she, astounding the company by rising abruptly to her feet. "I wish to dance!"

"Then dance you shall," sounded a most peculiar voice close by, before any member of the group could offer themselves, and turning she emitted a gasp of surprise to behold the Knight!

"Your offer comes most opportunely, sir," she replied with civility, recovering herself.

And ignoring the indiscretion of standing up with an utter stranger, she unhesitatingly bestowed her hand in his, peering up into the visor in an effort to see his face, but could discern nothing through the narrow slits. With-

146

out another word he guided her on to the floor to make up a set for the *contre-dance*, leaving her host of escorts to goggle after them in open-mouthed astonishment.

Christina instantly warmed to him, and as the dance commenced she cast another sly glance up at the visor—where she assumed his eyes were for she could feel them boring down upon her.

"If I may say so, Sir Knight, your agility is remarkable for one of your goodly size, not to mention the cumbersome armour you wear."

" 'Tis lightness of heart at dancing with one so fair," resounded from the helmet as he bowed low in the dance.

Christina emitted a peal of affected laughter as they parted momentarily. "Your dancing is excelled only by your tongue, it seems," she chided breathlessly when next they met.

"Come into the moonlight and I'll prove your words false."

"Fie on you, sir! I vow your audacity quite overwhelms me."

His manner suddenly changed as he swept her—in one quick movement—behind the shrubbery out of earshot of the guests, glancing about as if fearing he might be observed.

"Forgive my impetuosity. Time is of the essence and I cannot afford to waste it in idle dallying and flowery speeches," he hissed through the slits. "I am forced to speak out, but beg you to believe my intentions truly, truly honourable."

Christina cast a curious glance up at the forbidding visor.

"You know of my desperate plight, sir?"

"Nay, I know only that you seek a champion for your

147

cause," the mysterious voice rumbled from within, "and I would serve you right gladly."

She gasped in a mixture of surprise and excitement.

"Oh, good kind sir," she began, then broke off to peer anxiously through the leaves of the bushes to reassure herself that all was well. But all was not well! To her extreme vexation she spied Andrew's mother, Lady Sinclair, bearing down on them grave of countenance, and turned to alert her companion, but found to her stupefaction that he had vanished, as if into the very air.

CHAPTER ELEVEN

"La! There you are, child! I have searched everywhere for you this hour past. What are you doing tucked away in this dark corner screening yourself from view?" exclaimed Lady Sinclair as she drew within range, glancing round with quick darting movements like a hungry gull, her small beady eyes gleaming through her Elizabethan mask while her hawk-like nose gave a sniff or two as if trying to scent her quarry. "All alone, too?"

"What is it you want of me so urgently, your ladyship?" queried Christina, understandably ruffled.

"Andrew has kindly procured you some refreshment, and wishes you to join us."

To be reunited with Andrew was the last thing Christina wished at that precise moment—or any other—but there seemed no way of escape.

"Come along, Christina," her ladyship prodded briskly. "Dear Andrew has waited an age already. He will wonder what has become of us."

Pocketing her dejection, Christina rose to accompany Lady Sinclair down the room to where Andrew sat disconsolately in his Robin Hood outfit, the long peacock feather in his hat drooping in sympathy with his mood, and without as much as a glass of cordial in evidence. This omission his mother hastened to set right by insisting her son bring them some ratafia from the refreshment room at once, to which he readily agreed, leaping afoot, his depression banished.

Whilst he was gone, Lady Sinclair sat disconcertedly fanning herself, debating how to stimulate Christina into conversation. The girl was gazing round the ballroom resigned to her fate, idly contemplating the bevy of guests, doubting if her Knight would have sufficient courage to broach her in her present situation, when rescue came, even before Andrew had returned, in the form of a young beau named Horace Dingle, of such highly respected family that Lady Sinclair—try how she might—simply could not take exception. And so Christina was permitted to honour Mr Dingle for the gavotte, at the end of which she lost no time in running the Knight to earth by the fountains. To her surprise, he seemed even more eager to see her than she to see him. This time, they selected a more secluded spot lest their *tête-à-tête* be disturbed again.

He began by expressing regrets at having deserted her in such ungallant manner—yet did not venture an excuse. Howbeit, regardless of who he was, Christina was now ready to trust him for it was almost eleven o' clock, by which time she had anticipated being well *en route* to London. The hour-glass was running out. She had no choice but to throw herself on his mercy.

"Sir Knight," she ventured, devoured with apprehension, "y-you seem an honourable trustworthy gentleman—a-and as your offer is most sincere I-I trust you will not think ill of me if I presume. . . ."

"Yes? Yes?" boomed the voice enthusiastically, the owner sitting up agog, inspiring her to hurry on.

"I must place myself at further disadvantage, and crave your aid in saving the life of . . . of . . . one I l-love. Alas! time is my enemy also, and I must speak out as you have done . . . H-He is imprisoned in London . . . awaiting exe . . . cu . . . tion, indeed, may be a-at this . . . v-very moment . . . al-already. . . ."

A loud gasp and a cough echoed from inside the helmet ere he managed to cry out: "Say no more! Do not distress yourself! Beg of me whater'er you will—anything! My very life is yours to command!"

This was more than Christina had dared hope for! In fact, he was so fervent in his offer she got the strong impression he would have prostrated himself at her feet with servility had not it been for the armour and the deafening clatter it would have made.

"Oh, sir! Y-You are far too . . . too . . . generous!" she faltered, forcing an inflection in her voice to promote his sympathy still further, shielding her eyes behind her fan as if too overcome for words—but resuming immediately to save time. "I vow, Sir Knight, I should understand and accept gracefully should you feel obliged to deny me . . . it-it is much to ask . . . b-but I would have y-you . . . ride with m-me . . . to L-London . . . tonight . . . ere 'tis too late!"

An even louder gasp emanated from the helmet but this time of a peculiar asphyxiating sound, causing her to wonder if he also was about to depart this life—evoking her concern lest he do so before they had saved her be-

151

loved Dan. But the failing was brief, for when next he spoke he seemed to be in control of himself, and though his voice shook, it was with some degree of excitement.

"Then why do we dally? Come, we must get us gone!"

"Wait!" cried Christina, seizing his metal-clad arm to detain him. "We must tread warily! There are those who would stop us. Even at this very moment—"

"P-Pardon me, M-Miss Wansford," interrupted a timorous voice at this point. "B-But you promised to honour my h-hand for this d-dance . . . a-and you didn't come to get your cor-cordial. . . ."

To Christina's wild annoyance there stood Andrew, crimson-faced 'neath his mask of Lincoln green, nervously plucking at his sleeve, and ready to enlist the assistance of his forceful mother should she see fit to refuse him. Consequently, she would have suffered Andrew to lead her out but for the intervention of the Knight who at once claimed the dance his by right—a right or wrong the awkward Andrew was loth to gainsay.

So without more ado, the Knight led Christina into the dance once again, leaving Andrew to his own devices whilst they furthered their arrangements in step to the music. Throughout the dance Christina's eyes flitted anxiously round the room, raking the gathering for sight of Lord Stryde, wanting to keep him under surveillance lest he materialise of a sudden and catch her unawares. But the Marquess was nowhere to be seen.

Nevertheless, someone certainly did materialise—none other than her father who dumbfounded his daughter with his cavalier manner in interrupting the dance.

"Father!" she exclaimed, but Sir William Wansford showed keener interest in her partner as he bowed towards him to request politely:

"Surely Sir Launcelot will gallantly humour the whim of an old man who desires to dance with his daughter awhile?"

Contrary to this assumption, the Knight seemed about to object in no uncertain manner as his hand flew involuntarily to his sword-hilt to clench it ominously, his body tensed, until he eventually curbed his anger and, bowing stiffly with a click of his heels, stalked away.

For Christina, there was little to do but acknowledge her new partner.

"Father, I think you've offended him," she lamented, gazing after the retreating Knight.

"Have I, child? I am most terribly sorry. I assure you, it was not my deliberate intention. Is he a particular friend?"

Christina drew herself up quickly, gulping down her chagrin.

"Oh—er—no, of course not," she replied lightly, forcing a laugh. "Merely a casual acquaintance, nothing more." And she launched into frivolous conversation, hoping to convince him. "I was not aware that you danced, sir?" she continued in genuine surprise.

"Not as a rule, child," responded her father, his trembling legs striving to master the intricate steps. "However, I recall a little of this dance from my youth, and I was assailed with such an urge to be in your company that I temporarily forgot my manners just now. I trust you will forgive my indiscretion?"

His daughter was prepared to forgive him anything, having been denied his company for so long, and maintained her steady banter in order to banish all memories of the past wretched year from his mind.

But her father did not seem to be heeding her words at

present for his attention was focused elsewhere, and when she traced his line of vision, discovered it to be concentrated on the Sun God, as if wishing to attract his eye from the alluring Cleopatra he was engaged with. Seeming to sense his regard, Apollo suddenly glanced up, and though the look and nod which passed between them were imperceptible, they were nevertheless noticed by Christina whose misgiving increased amain.

Had her preferential treatment of the Knight been remarked? she gasped inside, her heart palpitating wildly. Had she inadvertently betrayed them both by her impulsiveness? If so, she must warn him and leave instantly.

The dance ended, and with difficulty she managed to elude her father (on pretext of adjourning to her boudoir to rest awhile)—to go in frantic search of the Knight, pressing through the swarms of guests, but ere she could reach him an elegant gentleman stepped unexpectedly out of the crowd to bar her path. It was done quite deliberately and she was about to command him to stand aside, assuming him to be intoxicated, when she recognised his Shakespearian costume, and his identity as Anthony Wilde, her future brother-in-law.

Whilst she sought to recover her countenance at his thus accosting her, he bowed courteously and astonished her even further by requesting her to dance with him, though with some embarrassment, his eyes deviating round the room to avoid her questioning gaze.

"Should not you be attending my sister, sir?" she queried, her stupefaction temporarily outweighing her annoyance at being yet again thwarted in her ambition.

"As you see, Miss Wansford," he sighed, gesturing towards the dancers, "your sister has deserted me in favour of Julius Caesar. Of course, if you'd rather not, then permit me to escort you to your father, or Lady Sinclair."

"No!" she burst out aghast, then hastily tried to cover up her reluctance. "I-I mean, I should be delighted to dance with you, but I have the headache and was about to adjourn to the gardens for a breath of air—"

"Then suffer me to accompany you thither," he cut in eagerly, proffering his arm. "I should also benefit from a breath or two of the—er—sweet night air."

Again Christina's warning mechanism sprang into action, crying out that conspiracy was afoot, prompting her to seriously question the dubious behaviour of those close to her during the past hour. No less than four attempts had been made to separate her from the Knight, which smacked of more than mere coincidence. First Lady Sinclair—then Andrew Sinclair—her father—and now, Anthony Wilde. Who would be next? Rebecca—or the instigator himself? Although she could sense Lord Stryde's subtle trap gradually closing in on her, she was not going to surrender without a fight. There was still time to escape, but she would need to act swiftly.

But it would seem that Mr Wilde was not going to be as easily discouraged as Andrew or her father, and so, yielding gracefully she accompanied him in the direction of the gardens; but before they had reached the door a piece of neatly folded paper was pushed into her hand, obviously a message, which she quickly tucked into the low-cut bodice of her gown, thus foiling any ideas her escort might have entertained about seizing it.

The gardens were quite well lit with Chinese lanterns, and as Christina and Mr. Wilde mingled with the couples parading about the groves, inhaling the balmy air, she continued to rattle her brain for some plausible excuse to rid herself of his cloying presence, deciding in the meantime, to amuse herself a little at his expense.

"Tell me, sir," she teased, feigning curiosity. "Is it a regular practice for Lord Stryde to select your partners for you, or does he occasionally permit you to select your own?"

This threw him off balance. "I-I don't quite f-follow you," he stammered, his eyes swivelling helplessly in the direction of the door, as if hoping his friend would come to his rescue.

"I think you do, Mr Wilde."

"It is only that he is anxious for your welfare—as indeed are we all——"

"So anxious that he would actually try to kill me?" she countered.

"K-Kill you!" he ejaculated in horror. "I-I don't believe it. I-It's a dream—your headache—the excitement of the occasion?"

"I see I am wasting my breath. It would seem that you are even more helpless than everyone else in resisting his Machiavellian influence."

"Miss Wansford," exclaimed he, coming to a sudden halt, "I cannot bear to listen to you slander Lord Stryde so unjustly without making some objection! I know my being a close friend of his gives you leave to doubt my word, but even so, you may accept it for what it's worth—that he has only your best interests at heart, and no matter what you say or do, I will not be convinced otherwise!" He struggled to master his emotions for it was a new experience for Anthony Wilde to lose his temper. "It isn't logical! Why should he act so?"

"I am surprised you, sir, of all people, should ask that!" she retaliated. "You have certainly changed your coat since the night of my arrival when you exhausted every vile word in the King's English to impress upon me his true character!"

"The—er—circumstances were quite different on the night you mention, Miss Wansford, when you prognosticated that you might possibly influence Lord Stryde to the good. It seemed laughable at the time, but it appears that I owe you a profound apology. I have never witnessed such a change in a man."

"Are you now trying to tell me that Lord Stryde is too good for this world, and considers me likewise?"

"I don't understand you."

"My meaning is plain enough, sir, though perhaps your perception is somewhat low on this auspicious day in your life. I refer, of course, to the tragedy in the barn."

He eyed her suspiciously. "I agree tragic, but I do not see how Lord Stryde could be held responsible?"

Christina circumspectly kept silent until a group of revellers passed them by and were well out of earshot.

"Your loyalty to his lordship does you credit, but alas, leaves me unmoved. Surely having murdered once it would be no problem for him to murder again?"

"M-Murder!" he spluttered.

"You seem shocked? La, sir, there is no need to keep up the pretence for my benefit, and no one can overhear. You may not realise that I am fully acquainted with the facts, and that the fourth Marquess met his untimely fate at the hands of his son."

At this Mr Wilde flared into the very personification of his name, evoking some alarm in Christina who hastily backed lest he strike her. But the awkward moment rapidly waned and he regained his self-control sufficiently to suggest they repair to the summer-house close by, in order that they might converse in complete privacy. Once inside and their masks removed, he resumed.

"You must guard your tongue, Miss Wansford. I don't know how you acquired your information, but I swear before God that it is utterly unfounded. I too am aware of the facts—the true facts—"

"Do you tell me that the old Marquess died naturally?" she asked with scepticism, exploring the interior of the summer-house, a hexagonal glass structure topped by a fluted cupola.

"Yes!" he declared forcefully, realising that she was drawing him deeper into the mire but unable to do much about it. "There is no reason to suspect otherwise."

This, Christina refused to believe. Not only had Lord Stryde made no attempt to deny the accusation but had openly confessed his guilt to her face. Obviously Mr Wilde was making a brave effort to shield his friend, unaware of how much she knew, and so she decided to fire a shot at random.

"If this is so, Mr Wilde, perhaps you could tell me why his Cousin Charles should seek to destroy him by proclaiming him guilty?"

The gentleman tugged irritably at the neck of his doublet and starched ruffle. "I—er—wasn't aware you were on such intimate t-terms with his—er—cousin," he muttered disjointedly, adding to her conviction.

"And knowing this, you still persist that Lord Stryde had nothing to do with the incident at Withey Hill?" she pursued, pausing by the open door of the summer-house to note, with a flush of satisfaction, the key nestling snugly in the lock.

"That is not for me, but the Marquess to divulge," Mr Wilde sought to extricate himself, wondering how the distasteful subject had ever arisen. "All I am at liberty to say is that Lord Stryde was nowhere near the barn at the time of the fire, and the hand that set it alight was not his, for he was with me at Barrington Hall where we spent the entire evening."

Christina glanced up suddenly, a gleam in her green eyes which—had Anthony Wilde known her a little better—would have forewarned him.

"Would you tell me, Mr Wilde, how did you know that *anyone* set the barn alight—and that it did not start by accident?"

Mr Wilde was stunned, confused and acutely embarrassed in that order, giving Christina abundant reason to feel pleased with herself, confirming her suspicions that he was purposely lying to protect his friend and wholly ignorant of the ring which she had in her possession as conclusive evidence.

"Your—er—s-sister?" he proffered hopefully.

Christina shook her head. "Rebecca was unconscious when the fire broke out. All she knows of the business is that she was roughly handled and struck on the head. You will need to stretch your ingenuity a little further, sir, for only two others know there was foul-play, namely, a prisoner in the condemned cell of Newgate Prison—and the person responsible. . . ."

Guilt was carved all over Mr Wilde's face as he mopped anxiously at his fevered brow with a white scented handkerchief.

"Y-You must appreciate my d-delicate position, M-Miss Wansford," he besought her, as if ready to dissolve through the hair-line cracks in the marble floor. "I-I am not sure how much you know of the dreadful occurrence, but no doubt you realise that duty curbs my tongue in

159

deference to Lord Stryde—I am therefore honour-bound to remain silent and respect his confidence."

Whilst he spoke, Christina—with her back to him—slyed the note from the bosom of her gown and read in the lantern—light, the following:

'I shall be waiting with a coach and six in the
Cypress Grove at midnight.'
Yr Knight.

"I understand perfectly, Mr Wilde," she returned pleasantly, trying to restrain the eagerness in her voice as she tucked the note away again. "And now, as time is rather pressing, I hope you will excuse me?"—and in one swift movement, ere he knew what she was about, she had whirled out of the door and turned the key in the lock, imprisoning him.

Christina hesitated no longer, but uplifted her gown and ran towards the servants' stairs and so up to her boudoir where—anticipating she might be obliged to make a hasty retreat—she had packed a bundle of effects to take with her on the expected journey to London, along with her accumulated plunder—whilst giving thanks to heaven that the summer-house was set in a remote part of the grounds and Mr Wilde's cries would not readily be heard.

Up the stairs she sped, wasting no time in draping her capuchin about her shoulders, and seizing her bundle was down again in seconds, and certain that it could not be far off midnight, set off towards the Cypress Grove where, true to his word, the Knight was awaiting her with a splendid coach and six. Evidently he was a gentleman of consequence—but who? Even when they were comfortably established in the vehicle, the team whipped into action and the coach underway, yet did he seem reluctant to reveal himself, and just as reluctant to talk.

They swept down the long driveway at a reckless pace, but before they had reached the Lodge a feeling of discomfort began to circulate within Christina which she refused to heed until they passed through the Main Gates and instead of turning right—turned left, clearly headed due west. This, she did not hesitate to communicate to her companion in armour who, to her intense horror, responded with a burst of fiendish laughter enough to freeze the blood in her veins, as it resounded ghoulishly inside the metallic mask—which, along with the rest of his armour, he now saw fit to remove.

Christina gasped in recognition. "M-Mr L-Liddell? . . . I-I don't under . . . stand . . . ?"

CHAPTER TWELVE

"Ye don't?" he questioned in obvious disbelief. "Ye still regard me as y'r good friend, eh?"

"Are we, or are we not bound for London?"

"London?" he chortled, rubbing his spatulate hands together with glee. "No, my Queen Guinevere, we are not bound for London."

"Then where are we bound for?" she demanded, growing exasperated.

"Ye like me game? Guess correctly and ye might merit a prize!"

Christina Wansford was not the sort of girl to fly into hysterics when anyone commanded—even adversity. Once accustomed to the idea that she was being abducted she simply summoned her dignity, flung up her head, and pierced him with her most frigid look.

"You have an odd sense of humour, Mr. Liddell," she stated in cutting tone. "If this is the outcome of some wager or other I am not amused. If you set me down immediately, however, no more will be said."

The chortle graduated to a loud cackle, goading her to wrathful humiliation at the way he had duped her.

"I demand you stop this coach at once!" she cried angrily. "At once d'you hear me?"

"I hear ye, sweet nymph," he smirked. "But I certainly do not intend stopping now with the winning-post in sight—especially when I've fair exhausted m'self plottin' and plannin'—though amply aided by y'r good self. B' George, the gods were on my side tonight, eh?"

"But why?—why? What's your reason?" she pressed him, confusion taking precedence. "Had I known who you were, sir, I would have still sought your help."

"Ye would?" he exclaimed in evident surprise, his bloated smug visage wiped sober. "Egad! I think ye mean it!" A curious gleam sprang into his lascivious eye. "You—er—don't, then, have safely stowed in y'r trinket-box a certain item—a ring, wrought in gold—befittin' a gentleman?"

"I do have such, sir, belonging to your cousin, Lord Stryde! But how do you know—"

"My cousin?" he broke in, puzzled. "Doth not it bear an inscription?"

"Yes, it is inscribed with the characters 'V' and 'B'— Valentine Barrington, which is how I know it belongs to the Marquess."

" 'V'?" he queried dubiously. "Is't not 'C'?"

" 'C'?"—it was now Christina's turn to query, every whit as puzzled.

"You perhaps do not know that I, also, am a Barrington? Charles Barrington, hence the 'C.B.'?"

"You!" choked Christina on a rapid intake of breath,

realising in a flash everything that this revelation implied. "N-No! Y-You can't be! L-Lord Wylton—"

"Is my step-father," he clarified with a grimace intended to be a smile. "My natural father was the younger brother o' the fourth Marquess, before he was mortally wounded in a duel, nigh thirty years agone. I informed y'r sister that the Wylton family name was Liddell, which she assumed was also mine—an assumption I saw no reason the redress."

Christina still shook her head, refusing to acknowledge the worst.

"No! I-It couldn't be you . . . s-set the b-barn on . . . f-fire!—it couldn't!"

This, he accorded with a pompous inclination of his frizzed head, evidently proud of what he had almost accomplished.

"Shall we say, 'twas all meticulously planned to safeguard my interests which ye came perilously near to ruinin'?"

Christina stared at him bewildered more than ever.

"Havin' a goodly perception of women and how their greedy little minds work, me connivin' coquette, I find it impossible to accept that y'r clever seduction of m' noble cousin was done bereft of all thought o' gain," he informed her, maliciously. "I really must felicitate ye, all the same, on acquirin' the unattainable—succeedin' where countless numbers have fallen by the way. Forsooth! Y'r approach must have been most original to bewitch him so."

"Bewitch!" ejaculated Christina. "If anyone is bewitched, sir, it's you! I have never heard such utter nonsense in all my life! The only feeling Lord Stryde and I have for each other is an intense mutual hatred," she remonstrated in outrage—racked with anguish to think that she was no nearer to saving Dan on account of this most recent folly.

He snarled suspiciously. "So much so, that he would go to the ridiculous lengths o'plannin' the nuptials?"

"You're insane! He's done no such thing! Anyway, I plan to marry someone else," she shouted furiously.

He indulged in a gruesome smile, unconvinced, though prepared to humour her.

"Ah, yes! Dan y'r highwayman, was't not? Gaspin' his last in the Tyburn jig!"

"H-How do you know this?" she burst out in alarm, but his smile merely broadened.

"It makes not a scrap o' difference how I know, Slayer o' Hearts—or how many lovers ye lay claim to. I have far too much at stake to let events run their course. Under law, I stand to inherit everything—everything—from Stryde's titles and Barrington Hall, right down to the last groat o' his fortune! And no money-grubbin' little trollop from York or anywhere else is going to jeopardise it! Ye won't be the first person I've taught a lesson for interferin' with me rights."

Christina's eyes widened, her mind racing ahead.

"Th-The old M-Marquess—y-you killed him!"

"Hold hard! Let's not be hasty!" he exclaimed, raising his hands as if to ward off the accusation. "I know ye'd like to believe so but alas, I must disappoint ye. Contrariwise, I had excellent reason for wantin' him alive, for he was on the threshold of disinheritin' his dissolute son, which should ha' proved most beneficial to m'self. But the old fool has to up with his heels at the vital moment!"

"H-He died naturally? L-Lord Stryde is truly innocent?"

Charles Barrington gave a careless shrug. "Why deny it now? By distortin' the truth slightly I sought to frighten ye away from Barrington Hall, but being the inquisitive obstinate female y' are ye refused to take the bait."

"And why tell me all this now?"

"Why not?" he returned with a magnanimous smile. "I don't mind satisfyin' y'r curiosity. It does no harm to grant y'r last requests—as they do with condemned prisoners."

Christina's heart leapt into her throat, but she kept rigid control of herself.

"C-Condemned p-prisoners?" she stammered on a note of dismay.

He leaned forward, a menacing gleam in his blood-shot eyes.

"As I said before, y're a nuisance! An obstacle in my way which must be removed. Had ye taken the sound advice ye were given and departed at the outset ye wouldn't now be in this situation, but no, ye had to thrust y'self in where ye weren't wanted, for which ye will now pay the ultimate penalty . . . death!"

With a groan Christina sank back into the crimson upholstery and closed her eyes to blot out his odious leering face, realising the futility of any effort on her part to effect an escape. To think she had been avoiding those around her all evening, who feared for her welfare, just to be in the company of this brute. And the Marquess . . . ! She cringed as she recalled her words to him only a matter of days ago. Full appreciation began to dawn on her of how well she had unwittingly cooperated with her abductor, concerning whose identity Lord Stryde seemed to be the only person aware—the one person who wanted rid of her. What difference would it make to him if she absconded with his rake-hell cousin, or Daring Daniel—or even the Devil himself? And if he was at this moment concerned about her absence—which was the height of improbability—might not he reasonably suppose that she was on her way to London as she had threatened?

"One thing I'll say for Val—he's certainly got an eye for the sex! By gad! He knows how to pick 'em!"

His greedy close-set eyes wandered over her as he licked his drooling lips, generating nothing in Christina but a sickening disgust.

"How could I have been so crazed as to think you a man of honour?" she spat at him.

"Didn't know I was a talented actor, did ye, O Flower o' my Delight? A little more practice and even Garrick will need to look to his laurels, eh?" he crowed, bestowing an affectionate pat on the helmet by his side. "There's no need to get frumpish just because ye were blinded by m' personal charm. Ye don't stand alone, y' know? Even Val himself was fooled—"

"Oh no!" she rounded on him. "Not your cousin! You didn't deceive him for a moment!"

He obviously did not hear her for he continued to simper to himself as they gathered even more speed.

"We'll see who'll be Marquess yet! I've outwitted him good and proper this time."

"And I say it is you, sir, that has been outwitted," she announced, determined to spike his guns. "By abducting me thus you actually do your cousin a favour, for he has wanted me out of his house ever since I first set foot in it!"

His eyes narrowed threateningly. "And I say, you lie!"

"I do not lie!" she flung back, confident in her assumption. "Even now, you are fulfilling his dearest wish, by ridding him of two very cumbersome birds."

He stared at her for some time, carefully weighing the possibility, before bursting into raucous laughter.

"Y'know, m'dear, I believe ye really think so. Egad! almost had me convinced too, except for one small thing. . . ."

"And what's that?"

"The nuptials."

"I tell you there's to be no nuptials—only my sister's!"

The conversation lapsed with this difference of opinion, and whilst he lolled back smiling confidently, Christina clung to the strap for support as the coach tore along the road at a suicidal rate, rocking on its axis.

"Wh-What are you going to do with me?" she ventured at length, reluctant to ask.

He sat up agog. "I have an excellent scheme!" he chuckled excitedly, like a child in anticipation of a treat.

"Not another," she repined.

"I too intend to rid m'self of two cumbersome birds—a cunnin' trap which Stryde won't get out of quite so easily."

"Lord Stryde?" she prompted, unable to perceive his meaning.

He paused to take a gleaming silver pistol from the holster by the window on his right, and held it up for her to see.

"Ye recognise it, m'dear?"

"Y-Yes," she replied doubtfully. "It's Lord Stryde's—it bears his crest."

"Exactly! Which will not only seal your fate, fair maid, but his also, when this weapon is discovered on the morrow beside y'r beautiful but very dead body on a lonely part o' the road—though where 'tis like to be found."

"Satan is an innocent babe compared to you!" she exclaimed in revulsion, conscious that support would be given to this by the servants at Barrington Hall who were well aware of the estrangement between their master and his elder ward.

He seemed to regard her comment as a compliment to himself and smiled in acknowledgement as she languished back on the squabs to offer up a silent prayer for a wheel to come unput, or the coach be waylaid, in order to give her some chance of escape. But no such intervention came. The monotonous beat of the hooves kept on and on, swaying her rhythmically in motion whilst he sat idly gazing round the coach, toying with his top waistcoat button as if tired of conversing.

Of a sudden he surprised her by uplifting part of the seat to reveal a secret compartment well-stocked with bottles and glasses. Selecting a bottle he filled a glass and proffered it—which she refused with a curt gesture. But he seemed unoffended and proceeded to indulge himself quite cheerfully alone.

"I see no reason why we shouldn't become better acquainted 'fore we needs must part, m'dear . . . There's no great hurry."

The wine was apparently having a mellowing effect.

"P'raps I shall postpone y'r departure to the after-life till we've enjoyed ourselves a little, eh?"

To Christina this prospect was even more abhorrent than the fate already planned, and without a second thought she made a dash for the door to fling herself out into the night and chance what may; but when she wrenched it open and saw undergrowth and trees flashing past her eyes at a terrifying rate, she hesitated briefly—but long enough for Charles Barrington to seize her by the cloak and haul her back inside, slamming the door and shattering the window-pane.

He swore a blasphemous oath. "Ye crazy bitch!—ye'd never survive!"

"Anything's better than suffering your revolting attentions!"

"Don't be selfish. Y're doomed to die anyway. What's the odds if I enjoy m'self first?"

Again he settled himself opposite, imbibing his wine—though bathing in it would be more accurate as most of it slopped over the glass to serve as further embellishment to his beflowered waistcoat. Throughout the ritual his eyes, now more blood-shot than ever, dilated at her whilst an ominous grin of pure lust sat transfixed upon his countenance.

"By the Devil! Ye grow more desirable with each drop. If I drink any more I'll devour ye in one mouthful and then regret it."

Christina flung him a look of scorn but he cared nought for her feelings, confident in the knowledge that she was wholly at his mercy and he was about to prove who was master. Staggering to his feet, he wiped a hand across his wet lips, striving to keep his balance as he relieved himself of waistcoat and sword, muttering: "We've wasted enough time talking, now we'll see some action."

He lunged at her but she sprang away with every muscle tensed.

"So! It's another game ye want, is it?"

He made another grab. "Nearly had ye that time, m' playful paramour—grumph!" he gasped suddenly, as her foot plunged into his abdomen. "You she-devil!" he yelled. "Keep still! Ye'll have us in the ditch! Why not give in gracefully? Y're only makin' things worse for y'self, because when I *do* catch ye. . . ."

But Christina had no intention of giving in and to convince him she snatched up the winebottle and threw it at his head, sending him crashing to the floor. She blenched at the volley of obscenities which issued from his lips as he stumbled to his feet, the coach rocking with the impact of his fall.

"If you want to play rough, mistress, I can play rough too," he growled through his teeth, dusting himself down with one hand and taking up his sword with the other.

Christina shrank into the velvet in horror, bethinking her end was coming sooner than anticipated, not daring to breathe as the sword-point brushed against her throat. Then, with one flash of the deadly blade he slit her dress from top to bottom. She unleashed an ear-splitting scream for it seemed as if he had sliced right through her flesh—which made him crow with laughter before he tossed away the weapon and dragged her ruthlessly down onto the seat. As his slavering lips smothered hers she was overcome with nausea at his heady perfume and the stench from his decayed teeth, and his foul breath, as he panted in anticipation of what was to come. This urged her to struggle more frantically, screaming for help when her breath allowed—and seemingly not in vain for all at once a resounding pistol-shot was heard outside, borne distinctly to their ears through the broken window. Not long after this the coach lurched to a halt, hurling them both onto the floor with a jarring thud.

Rapidly collecting herself together, Christina screamed again with all the breath she had left, battling to free herself from Charles Barrington's hold until he reluctantly let

171

her go with a round curse upon the intruder. Stumbling to her feet, she made a grab at the door as it was jerked open from the outside, revealing the one person in the world she never expected—tall, black, and extremely hostile.

"Dan!" she gasped, throwing herself into his arms, unable to give voice to the ineffable joy surging inside her.

Where her Knight of the Road had yet again sprung from she had not the strength nor wits to ponder. All she could do was cling to him, burying her face in the haven of his shoulder as his blazing eyes swept over her ravaged state.

He said nothing, but swung her to the ground to clutch her shivering body to him with his left arm, while his right aimed a pistol at Mr Barrington who was once again struggling to his feet from an ungainly position upon the floor. Although the highwayman's fury smouldered like a volcano, it was little compared to the indescribable hatred manifest on the face of his foe.

"How the hell did you get here?" snarled Barrington, incensed.

But all he got in reply was a curt command to climb down and bring his sword with him.

"Sword!" he echoed in surprised indignation. "I'll be damned 'fore I'll cross swords with you out in this wilderness at one i' the morn!"

"Very well," returned the other, calmly. "Then this ball goes through your brain here and now." And levelling the pistol steadily at Mr Barrington's head he prepared to fire, thus prompting Barrington to vacate the coach with astounding alacrity, sword in hand.

"Dan!" cried Christina aghast. "Y-You aren't going to fight?"

"Ye do well to protest, m'dear," sneered Barrington. "Ye obviously value his life more than he does."

"Can't we just leave quietly without further unpleasantness?" she petitioned, devoured with fear for his precious being—having had it but just restored to her.

But all she got in reply was a request to stand aside and keep the pistol—which he handed her—trained on the unconscious coachman lest he should rouse.

"I object!" shouted Charles Barrington.

"You are in no position to object!" came the acid rejoinder.

"What's to stop her firing that thing at me?"

"Nothing—but why waste time arguing the point when you won't be living long, anyway?"

"We'll see about that, ye cocky devil!" snapped the other, flexing his sword-arm as he rolled up his silk shirt sleeves. "We'll see how confident you are when I've done with ye!"

And without warning he lunged to the attack, expecting to catch his opponent unawares; but the highwayman leapt nimbly aside, avoiding his enemy's blade by inches, and whipping forth his own sword, turned to engage the next attack, tossing aside his hat. Mr Barrington launched at him again, not granting him the chance to discard his heavy surtout and thus put them on a more even par, and the fight began in earnest, the ring and clash of steel echoing throughout the deathly night stillness.

Contrary to his expectations, Charles Barrington did not find the going easy, finding his adversary in much better condition after his long ride than he had first thought, therefore the bout would last a while longer, but the ultimate end would be the same . . . twenty inches of cold steel through his black heart.

But the conflict raged on—cut and thrust, feint and parry—both evidently born fencers, tireless in their efforts, while Christina's green eyes shuttled back and forth from the unconscious coachman to the duel to the death between the two men—the one she loved passionately, and the one she loathed just as intensely—her body rigid with suspense as she followed the flashing blades in the coach lights. Never had she seen Dan fence so well—but then, she had never really seen him fence at all, and realised how she had grossly under-rated him. Several times she had noticed Charles Barrington make a cowardly pass which Dan had deftly countered—to her sheer astonishment—only just managing to stop herself crying out.

Meanwhile, Charles Barrington was slashing away at his opponent, beginning to doubt the certainty of his impending victory as he continued to encounter calm opposition to his every move; furthermore, he was now feeling the strain of his surplus weight and was therefore not as light on his feet as his foe—who seemed to be a direct descendant of Will o' the Wisp—and who by now had somehow rid himself of his coat. In desperation Mr Barrington decided to inject his infallible strategem into the fray, and slying forth his snuff-box, awaited an opportune moment, then flung the entire contents of the box in the other's face.

Christina gave a piercing shriek and averted her eyes, too terrified to look, but the highwayman seemed well able to cope with the unorthodox fencing methods of his rival and nimbly evaded the clouds of snuff borne on the night air, and for a while assumed command, driving the other slowly back. Both by now were showing signs of exhaustion, their breathing laboured, when a sudden groan sounded from the coachbox which gained Christina's immediate attention. She dragged her eyes from the conflict to range the pistol steadily on the awakening coachman who, despite cracked cranium, did not take long to grasp the situation and, anxious to avoid a hole in his brain, decided to remain mumchance lest the lady should nervously fire first, and question him afterwards.

Mr. Barrington, hearing the groan from his hired hand, called out irascibly: "Don't just sit there, you son of a whore! Seize the pistol! That spineless jade won't shoot—aagh!"

He was abruptly silenced as the point of Dan's sword pierced his left shoulder.

"Perhaps that will teach you to respect the gentler sex, you overgrown swine!"

With a yelp of pain Charles Barrington retreated a pace or two, clutching his wound to give it a cursory examination; but once assured that it was not serious he hurled himself into the fight with renewed vigour, hacking unmercifully at his enemy—who was forced to give ground in deference to the other's superiority in sheer physical strength.

It was not long, howbeit, before Barrington was granted retribution for his pinked shoulder as at this point the coachman summoned courage to kick at the lantern nearest Christina, plunging her into sudden darkness, then sprang down from the box ere she realised what was afoot to wrench the pistol from her startled grasp. This caused her to scream out yet again as she struggled with him, momentarily distracting the highwayman who could not resist an anxious glance in her direction—which opportunity his enemy seized to lacerate his right arm with one

175

fell stroke. In a flash, Dan transferred his sword to his other hand even though he was not allowed one second's respite to check the ugly wound by the other who drove him relentlessly back in a rigorous attack. It was only by bounding up on to the step of the coach and plunging his right foot into Barrington's brawny chest, propelling him back into the undergrowth, that he managed to regain part of his former control, flashing a look at Christina to ensure all was well ere he leapt upon his foe in deadly earnest in a final bid to end the duel, realising that his own strength was about to fail at any moment.

Christina, having managed to outwit the coachman, once again had him under threat of the pistol, striving to keep her attention focused on him instead of the desperate battle for survival between the two—both of whom were now suffering wounds of varying degrees, making it indeed a duel to the death in grim determination on either side as the pair of blood-bathed figures engaged for the final assault, each equally intent on dealing the death-blow and killing the other.

When it came it was swift and sure, for Charles Barrington's attention was centred wholly on his opponent's movements, heedless of his own. This proved to be his own downfall as his staggering feet encountered the fallen lantern, and losing his balance he stumbled heavily on to the point of his adversary's sword which penetrated his stomach up to the hilt. His eyes protruded from his head in horror and disbelief as he lurched forward towards Dan, who drew his weapon free then collapsed against the coach, heaving for breath while Barrington fell unconscious at his feet.

With an inarticulate cry, Christina flew to her highwayman's side, throwing her arms about his racked body in frantic concern but overwhelming relief that it was all over and he was alive—leaving the coachman to stand nonplussed, unsure whether to stay, or risk making a dash for freedom.

"Oh, Dan!" she breathed anxiously. "Are you much hurt?"

"Noth . . . ing . . . ser . . . ious," he gasped, dropping the sword to examine the wound in his arm—the worst he had sustained—while Christina tore a strip from her already tattered gown to bind it up.

When he had assured her that he was quite well enough to ride, she went to retrieve his horse and clothing, but on turning to make her way back her feet froze in their tracks, for Charles Barrington—whom they had presumed dead, and forgotten about—was struggling up on one elbow, still clutching his weapon and determined to make a last attempt to avenge himself on his killer, who stood with his back towards him wholly oblivious to the evil afoot.

Christina stood stricken, petrified with fear, and at this critical time found herself unable to utter a syllable. When she did, she knew it was already too late.

"Dan! Look out—behind you!" she shrieked, seeking feverishly about her person for the pistol which she now realised she must have dropped in the excitement.

Even as she called out the sword pierced his side, and as his enemy fell again to the ground overcome with the strain, he dragged the weapon down with him, leaving an ugly gaping slash in Dan's right side. Unleashing a spine-chilling version of his customary insane laugh, Charles Barrington choked of a sudden, coughing up great spurts of blood ere he expired from the present world into the next—rolling over on to his back with eyes glazed and staring up at the heavens, his thick lips drawn back from his rotten teeth in a hideous ghoulish grin.

With a groan Dan clutched his side and sank slowly to his knees, Christina reaching him in time to clasp his injured body to her before he should fall prone upon the dusty highway.

Glancing about her in wild appeal for the coachman whom she thought might be willing to turncoat and help her for a handsome bribe, she discovered to her further dismay that she was completely alone—deserted, miles from anywhere in the dead of night, with the man she loved dying in her arms, the coachman having decided to take to his heels whilst he was still able.

CHAPTER THIRTEEN

For one crucifying moment Christina felt a madness welling up inside her—growing, growing, into Gargantuan proportions, which she battled manfully to suppress, for succumbing to it would not help save Dan's life. Instead, although close close to hysteria, she set about what was to be done calmly and sensibly, taking each task in her stride; binding up the grievous wound in his side with the remains of her gown, first of all, and enveloping herself in her cloak, while shaking off the nausea which threatened at the sight of so much blood. Her next trial was to mount him on the horse—or at least get him over the beast's back somehow. Flashing a wistful glance at the cosy interior of the coach she firmly rejected the overwhelming urge to take it, appreciating the danger in doing so, for as things stood there was nothing to connect them directly with the killing of Charles Barrington. True, there was the coachman, but there was little likelihood of his being able to recognise them again, even if he should want to.

Thus decided, she gathered together all incriminating evidence, including the Marquess's pistol, simply because she did not wish to see him wrongfully accused of his cousin's death. Throwing Dan's coat across the horse, she set about lifting up Dan himself—which proved no mean task, as she struggled with his dead weight over her shoulder trying hard not to bump him—and might have proved impossible had she been a female of less robust build. Then, collecting her bundle from the coach, she mounted behind him and with a final glance round the macabre little scene, set off slowly along the road, racking her brain over her next problem—where she was to take him, for Barrington Hall was clearly out of the question.

However, it may have been due to her own subconscious thoughts, or divine intervention, that she found herself traversing familiar ground along a certain lane where she had oft-times ridden with Dan, and passed what had once been a homely picturesque cottage which had claimed her interest, for it was now quite deserted, showing all the obvious signs of neglect, including an overgrown garden. It was here that Christina finally drew rein, rejoicing inwardly, for the cottage suited her needs to perfection, being secluded—sheltered on three sides by rambling saplings and undergrowth—and the last place where anyone would think of looking.

Swiftly, she dismounted and went inside to find the cottage consisted simply of two rooms—one for living and one for sleeping—and was further pleased to find it quite habitable from what she could distinguish in the darkness, though dusty and boasting the barest essentials and nothing more. These included an old threadbare couch, a warped wooden table, two rickety chairs, a stool with a missing leg, and a small cupboard wherein she discovered a tinder-box and rusty lantern containing a stump of tallow candle. Lighting the lantern, she then inspected the second room which embraced nought but a double-size bed complete with ragged palliasse (eagerly displaying its straw), a set of crudely made drawers, and another chair.

Dan was then conveyed to the bed, admittedly with difficulty, and the horse was settled for the night in the yard behind the cottage, after which Christina donned her only gown, of yellow cambric, and commenced work in earnest—not stopping to marvel at her inexhaustible supply of strength, having endured one of the worst ordeals in anyone's life.

But there was much to be done; seeking wood for the fire, water from the pump to heat in the huge black cooking-pot, and tearing up her petticoat into lengths of bandages. Placing hot water and bandages by the bed, she then proceeded to bathe the patient's wounds, commencing with the major one in his side, pausing ever and anon to check his breathing, and last of all, binding them up to the best of her poor ability.

Although she had not eaten for several hours, she found she had no appetite, perhaps just as well, for as to be expected the cottage had not a scrap of food on its dusty shelves.

It was now that Christina's nerves threatened to take possession of her as the full import of Dan's distressing condition and her own wretched plight descended upon her. Granted, the situation could have been much, much worse and he already dead, as the Marquess had foretold, but this was of little consolation at this time. Though she was resolved to stay awake as she sat vigil by the bed, she suffered lapses, dozing at intervals to rouse of a sudden and severely rebuke herself for relaxing her watch, until early morning when tiredness eventually overcame her and she slept soundly for several hours. On stirring, she was aghast to see the sun high in the sky and hurriedly shook herself awake to survey the patient; but he lay in the same condition, apparently not having moved all night.

Whilst he yet slept, she busied herself cleaning up the cottage, then journeyed to a farm a good mile distant to seek provisions, including a flagon of home-brewed ale, and tallow to make candles—thankful that the farmer's dame did not suspect who she was or ask any awkward questions (though considerable interest was shown in the horse by the labourers)—as both farm and cottage were situated on the Marquess's estate and undue curiosity could have aggravated her problem.

Appreciating that the only answer to her anxiety was hard work, Christina drove herself relentlessly, but even so, found it impossible to blot out the anguish consuming her—not only concerning Dan, but her father, and Rebecca—and the Marquess! . . . What would he now think of her? Shame and bitter remorse racked her being at the accusations she had levelled against him—most of all, his cousin's heinous act at Withey Hill—to think that she had actually cherished his guilt in her heart all these months—and would never be given the opportunity to salve her conscience by begging his pardon.

Each time Christina tended her patient she found her eyes wandering to the fateful mask—re-picturing in her mind the horror it concealed, aware that the time would come when she must needs remove it, and unable to determine how she would ever summon the overwhelming courage to do so.

During the night and the following day she spent her time by the sickbed, leaving it only when necessity demanded and hastening back to find Dan always in the same condition—until midway through the next night when he rudely awakened her, in the throes of a high fever. Christina was frantic with concern as she lit the lantern and made a hurried inspection of the wounds, relieved to find them not unduly inflamed, and so, replaced the dressings with a cold compress.

At noon the following day the fever waned as unexpectedly as it had risen, and he drifted back into a heavy coma, but leaving her more convinced than ever that he was in desperate need of medical attention—which was quite out of the question for the only doctor she knew of thereabouts was the Marquess's own physician, whom she did not dare summon.

For the rest of the day she wandered aimlessly about the cottage, picking things up, putting them down, unable to eat, drink, or even settle in one place for more than a few seconds gnawing at her fingers, and seizing upon the most trivial of tasks to save her sanity. Never had she endured such unbearable anguish, such soul-searing torment; and at night it was worse, for she found herself leaping up from her chair by the bed, quivering with anxiety each time an agonised groan escaped his lips.

The next day saw Christina worn to a shadow. Dan still lay unconscious and the unbelievable strain of the past four days had taken a severe toll from her looks and temperament. She sat as usual by the bed, watching him sleeping whilst she fidgeted with anything to hand, certain that she could not possibly endure another night like the last. At regular intervals she would wring out the cloth and replace it on his forehead like a clockwork figure, her fingers encountering the mask each time, urging her to remove it until she was consumed with guilt and wrestled violently with her conscience, battling to muster sufficient stamina, and choke down the overpowering revulsion which overcame her at the very thought of the ghastly features that lay beneath.

Howbeit, even as she stood thus arguing the matter, some outside force again intervened to decide the issue—in the form of Dan himself who, at that precise moment, began to toss about in an attack of delirium, and flinging a hand up to his face, tore the offending mask away with a violent gesture, casting it aside as if thankful to be disburdened of it, revealing features beneath which, far from being horribly distorted, were undeniably handsome—so handsome, in fact, that Christina herself would have readily agreed. Why then, was she devoured with more abhorrence than if his face had indeed been mutilated beyond belief? Why did she stagger back to the door, her entire being refusing to acknowledge the indisputable evidence of her eyes? Undoubtedly because the countenance she gazed upon was that of the person she dreaded most in the world—whose wickedness and deceit were a byword in the county, excelled only by Charles Barrington, and who filled her with the same dire feeling she now experienced when it duly penetrated her numbed brain that Dan her highwayman was none other than her erstwhile guardian, the Marquess of Stryde.

Christina stood transfixed for some time, her eyes suffused with horror, shaking her head from side to side, denying that which was painfully evident, her back cleaving to the door in an effort to strain as far away from him as possible until she wrenched it open and stumbled blindly into the living-room to throw herself down upon the worn couch by the window in a paroxysm of grief, cramming her fists into her mouth to stop herself screaming out loud, her teeth biting into her flesh until they drew spots of blood, at intervals pounding the seat to alleviate the terrible remorse. Her emotions waged such fierce war on her power of reason that for one frightening moment it would seem she would indeed be bereft of it— but oddly enough she did not cry. Tears were too inadequate! Instead, following the initial outburst she just lay paralysed with despair, weak and utterly defeated, unable to withstand the blow of this accursed knowledge on top of all else. All she knew was that her magic bubble had burst. Her Black Knight had crumbled to dust before her eyes, and she was now completely alone as if he had indeed been hanged. Nothing was real any more—only the agonising heartache, and the stranger lying in the next room.

Why? Why should anyone go to such extreme lengths solely to gratify an insatiable thirst for cruelty and vengeance on her sex? she kept asking herself. What satisfaction did he derive from grinding her down to this pitiable state? But more than this, how could she have been such a blind fool—so deceived? And above all, how could the two possibly be one and the same man? Dan, who had been a wholly different being—kind, understanding, even humble on occasion, and . . . passionate—all qualities utterly alien to the Marquess.

She sat up to gaze chin on fist through the lattice upon the overgrown garden, with the little sundial in the centre submerged amongst grass and weeds, her sunken eyes following the crooked path to the gate, bethinking both cottage and garden a ludicrous contradiction of Lord Stryde's lavish way of life. And as she sat thus she found her mind travelling back over the past to relive her wonderful moments with the highwayman, wishing she had known then what she now knew for she would have dissolved the partnership instanter instead of pouring out her heart at his feet.

Yet each time Christina sought to revile him, she found his passionate declaration of love rearing its head to spike her satisfaction. Had that too been a sham—a pretence—and his kisses, kisses of Judas?

Although this sudden revelation solved many problems for her, alas! it created many new ones, which only he himself could explain. Blinded as she was by wrathful indignation and hurt pride, she had omitted to ask herself one very vital question, namely, why a man bent so determinedly on her destruction should risk his life so often and willingly on her behalf? The nearest she ventured to this was to confess it her fault he lay in his present state and acknowledge it her duty to do all in her power to help him recover, and thus fulfil her obligation. What the future now held in store she could not bear to think, for the very word 'marriage' was a dagger in her breast.

She postponed the agony of having to tend him as long as possible, but was eventually forced to accede to the distasteful task, and rose from the couch, smoothing out her gown and patting her coiled hair into place. She was now perfectly calm, and firmly decided that everything must continue as before. Her personal feelings would be shelved for the moment and not allowed to interfere, for there would be ample opportunity to avenge them when he was sufficiently well to defend himself.

Contrary to her former visits, this time when she entered the room she was praying ardently that he would remain unconscious, for she would die with humiliation should he chance to waken during the process. Timidly, she approached the bed, eyeing him cautiously to reassure herself that he still slept, then placing the tray (improvised from the cooking-pot lid) upon the chair by the bed, set to work. Apprehensively, she removed the old dressing in order to bathe the wound in his side, when she stopped short and caught her breath. Had he flinched slightly—or was it her imagination? She flashed a look at his face but it was as before, expressionless and deathly pale, with eyes closed. Swallowing hard, she resumed her task with deft fingers, working as quickly and gently as she could, to finally heave a sigh when the harrowing job was done.

Picking up her 'tray', she was about to leave, but despite herself found her eyes drawn instinctively to those arresting features which appeared even more appealing in his present helplessness, the face she knew so well yet little over a year ago had never even seen . . . the sweeping black lashes, and long raven hair which had fallen loose from its rigid pigtail and caressed his wan cheeks, unusually pallid and strangely enhancing, his mouth not curled in a sneer, but relaxed—and as she stood thus rapt in contemplation of her patient, his eyes opened.

Christina leapt back as if bitten, precipitating pot-lid and contents upon the bare stone floor with a clatter—to rapidly pull herself together and manage to stammer an enquiry into his condition whilst hastily gathering up the pieces of earthenware bowl—following which she nervoulsy slopped ale into a crude tin mug and held it to his lips. The Marquess took three lingering sips, regarding her the while over the rim of the mug, and when he did eventually respond it was to tell her only what she had already suspected, that he felt deathly. He then fell back into oblivion and remained so for the rest of the day.

This brief return to consciousness was the first of a sequel of such bouts which continued throughout the night, the length of time between each gradually diminishing, until late the next morning when he remained awake long enough to partake of a bowl of gruel, spoon-fed to him by his nurse, who found it her worst experience so far. A pregnant silence prevailed the while, her hands trembling visibly despite stringent efforts to control them, due to her patient's steadfast gaze which never left her face. The only time conversation passed betwixt them was when she enquired if he desired her to summon his physician, and perhaps send a message to Barrington Hall to allay anxiety, to which he responded that she was everything he required in a physician, seemingly competent enough, and that he failed to see how any message could be sent to his home when there was obviously no means of having it delivered, adding that it was immaterial as he would be returning in a day or two.

Christina thought the idea utterly absurd. He would be exceedingly lucky to quit the bed at all, let alone in two days. But she chose not to voice her protest lest it excite him, and so returned to her work.

True to her word, Christina resolutely carried out her duties during the ensuing days, caring for her noble lord's every need—he proving surprisingly docile, though he gradually waxed stronger, doing exactly as he was bid, and suffering her to tend his wounds, wash him, comb his unruly locks, dose him with physic (personally recommended by the farmer's wife to cure all manner of ills) and even shave him (a razor being one of several useful items she had procured from a tinker chancing by) without a breath of protest escaping his lips. But though she continued in her solicitous attention it was, even so, administered with a cold reserve accompanied by a disconcerting silence, which the Marquess made no attempt to break until one day, after doing justice to a platterful of ham and eggs fresh from the farm, when he sat up, surveying her every movement as she tidied bed and room.

"Well? I presume we are now in hot pursuit of holy orders?" he queried casually, but intending to provoke.

Christina stiffened but went on with her work, wedging her tongue firmly between her teeth as she realised he was about to commence the attack.

"Or mayhap you favour the scintillating companionship of some decrepit dowager duchess?"

She thumped vigorously at the worn straw mattress until it looked about to fall apart, refusing to be drawn out.

"You seem to enjoy your work," he went on to observe with interest. "Not many menials do now-a-days." He paused in vain for a reply, so continued undaunted. "Should you desire the customary character I trust you will not hesitate to approach me, that is, unless you plan to further your criminal interests?"

The Marquess remained quite undeterred by the silence for he was noting with a degree of satisfaction the brewing storm in her heavy-handed manner and flushed countenance.

"By the faith! The merest suggestion of your association with the notorious Black Dan should gain you instant popularity in Hell's Den."

Christina swung round, eyes blazing, struggling to hold back the tempest within her.

"Yes?" he prompted infuriatingly, before her self-control won the day. "You can't pretend indefinitely that I don't exist."

"Is there anything further that you require, my lord?" she demanded, her bosom heaving turbulently, as his affable veneer suddenly cracked.

"Why do you stay?" he thundered at her. "Why?"

"Do not excite yourself—you may develop another fever—"

"Then speak, damn you!"

Christina advanced to the door lest she say something she might afterwards regret, but he ordered her back, complaining that his bed was uncomfortable. And so she mutely obeyed, and he resumed his inquisition.

"Why do you choose to preserve my worthless life thus, if the world would be the better with me out of it?"

"You would not lie here in this critical state, my lord, had I not acted so irresponsibly, therefore the least I can do in return is try to nurse you back to your customary health. I shall leave when you are fully recovered and not before."

"For which I should be profoundly grateful!" he snapped.

"On the contrary, my Lord Marquess!" she rounded on him, unable to endure his taunting any longer. " 'Tis I who must bear that burden! Since you have saved my life on countless occasions—and at grave danger to your own—I consider it ample punishment for me to be forced to live with the knowledge for the rest of my days, without having to lay my gratitude at your feet."

"I don't want your confounded gratitude!" he rasped with contempt.

"Furthermore, I am not blind to the fact that your

most recent sacrifice was not wholly on my account, that you had a deal more to lose than a wayward ward!" she flashed back.

"Meaning?"

"That you were well aware before you took the gamble precisely what was at stake—not only your life, but your entire inheritance which your cousin had planned to seize—"

"And which has been his sole ambition since he first drew breath, but which is not," he added with emphasis, eyeing her challengingly, "the prime reason why I lie here in my present lamentable condition."

There fell a tense pause, Christina trying to deny the ray of hope which had broken through her darkness of despair, all at once yearning to know this prime reason, but too proud to ask.

"I-I cannot discuss the matter any further," was all she could say, at length, "until you are fully recovered."

"Meanwhile, can't you be a trifle more sociable?" he ventured, extending the olive branch.

"No," she replied, turning her back to him, unable to meet those dark devouring eyes lest they weaken her resistance to his evil influence and cloud her mind to the extent of his treachery.

"If you're so cut up at losing your blasted highway-man," he shouted, losing patience, "why don't you rant and rave about the place—or burst into tears like any normal female?"

"To what purpose, my lord?"

The Marquess gave up with a sigh of futility. "Is it yet time to attend me?" he asked with resignation.

Christina inwardly rebelled at the suggestion 'neath the present cloud of acrimony.

"I—I'll tend you later when you are sleeping. I shan't disturb you."

"It isn't your usual practice to wait until I'm asleep," he pointed out scathingly, as she made to take up the utensils.

"N-No, b-but it will be more convenient, a-and . . . less . . . less. . . ."

"Less what?"

". . . l-less p-pain . . . ful."

"For whom?"—without warning he seized her by the wrist, dragging her to him. "What's happened to you? It didn't pain you to grovel at my feet begging me to take you, offering yourself—or to lie in my arms demented with desire!"

"Must you remind me of my folly, sir?" she burst out in anguish, suddenly fully aware of the depths of his deceit.

"Where's that overwhelming love you bore me then?" he persisted, gradually, mercilessly, breaking her down.

"I-It wasn't you I loved—"

"Wasn't it? Whom then?"

Christina wrestled violently to free herself, realising her self-control was going, but he held on relentlessly.

"No!" she cried out wildly. "You are not the man I loved! He was wonderful, sincere—and human!"

"That was me, woman!" he flung back, exasperated. "You talk as if I were two separate beings!"

"You are only one being," she sobbed, finally wrenching her arm free and fleeing to the door. "The one I loved is dead!"

With that she swept out, slamming the communicating door into the living-room, to fall against it, her heart pounding, striving to regain her composure. She had not meant to shout at him with such conviction—or even shout at him at all. He was still extremely ill and ought not to be disquieted in any way—but he had tormented her beyond endurance. In future, she would need to take greater care to be on her guard.

This precaution, however, proved unneccessary as following the explosive incident the Marquess's manner changed. Although he continued to make steady progress he ate little, but had frequent recourse to the ale-flagon and made no further attempt to converse, preferring to spend most of the day deep in meditation, at times so absorbed in his thoughts that he failed to respond to her aloof enquiries regarding his state of health. And eventually, he lapsed completely into his old self, ignoring her altogether except for the occasional glance of languid indifference, so much so, that Christina began to suspect that he actually deemed himself the offended party. The tense atmosphere—to which he now seemed wholly impervious—was even more intolerable than before, yet despite her difficult position she rallied on undeterred, repaying him with cold civility.

Her earlier desire to storm at him and avenge her wounded pride and broken heart had since given place to bitterness. Had he attempted to vindicate his actions with some plausible explanation her burden of grief might have been easier to bear, but he had not. His prolonged silence more than confessed his guilt—not that she now cared what had been his motive for such vile abuse of her love and trust, for it was sufficient in itself that he had dragged her down to suffer this degradation. All she wanted was to quit his presence and house for ever, and seek seclusion in her beloved Yorkshire, with her father.

However, three days hence, events took a dramatic

turn when she carried his mid-day meal in to him as usual, to find the bed empty. Placing the improvised tray by the bed the better to investigate, the door mysteriously closed behind her and she spun round—horrified to see him fully dressed including surtout and boots, with cocked hat in hand, leaning heavily on the door-knob.

"L-Lord St-Stryde!" she gasped in alarm, wondering how on earth he had managed to dress himself without her knowledge. "What are you doing out of bed! Your wound—it isn't yet healed."

"Nevertheless, I am leaving," he apprised her, laconically. "Consider your obligation fulfilled."

"L-Leaving?" she stammered, though it looked perfectly obvious.

"However, before I go there is a certain matter I should like to clear up, though it may mean pain and unpleasantness—"

"Please," she begged in genuine concern, as he still looked dreadfully weak. "A-At least, be seated."

"There is no cause for anxiety. Rest assured I feel reasonably fit," he tried to convince her somewhat hesitantly, seeming to give the lie to his words by gripping the door-knob the tighter. Inhaling deeply, he asked quietly: "Where would you like me to begin?"

Christina averted her eyes, nonplussed, inwardly rankled at being caught off-guard on such a vital issue about which, a few days ago, she had longed to say so much, yet now at the crucial moment, found the relevant words maddeningly evasive.

"Th-There is nothing I wish to discuss," she murmured, childlike.

The Marquess threw her a sardonic look. "Do you prefer to go on ignoring it? Pretending it never happened?"

194

"I don't see how you could possibly justify your actions!" she blurted out, reproachfully.

"Be that as it may, in all fairness, I think you should at least let me try."

"Haven't I suffered enough? Must you continue to torture me?"

"I fail to see what you have to complain about," he remarked irritably, striving to conceal the blazing agony in his side. "I am the wounded party in more ways than one."

"You, the wounded party!" she flared. "After what you've done to me? The lies, deceit, cowardice? Because I was fool enough to lay my heart at your feet, you had to salve your pride by grinding it into the dust, knowing how much I loved you . . . I-I was your s-slave . . . I worshipped you. . . ." A lump rose in her throat and she swallowed hard. "H-How could you repay me thus?"

"I shall state my reasons when I am given a chance—"

"What reasons could possibly excuse such vile abuse of my inexperience? My youth? My innocence? The lies which tripped glibly from your tongue? Having to flee the country to evade arrest? The reward on your head? Your pitiful scarred face—even going to the extreme of having false disfigured features made from painted chicken-skin to deliberately deceive me? And last of all, the great confession of love? What a performance! It even excelled your cousin's portrayal of St. George!" She swung away, unable to face him at the poignant reminder, resting her burning cheek on the bedpost. "I-I could forgive you anything—anything—" she murmured brokenly, "—but not the deception of that declaration. You seemed so sincere, so ardent and tender, as if you treasured every kiss, every gesture the same as I . . . but instead—" here she rounded on him afresh, fevered with resentment—"you hurled it in my face, abused it and condemned it—no doubt to prepare me for this bitter disillusionment!"

She paced round the bed, wringing her hands agitatedly.

"Had I been an experienced woman of the world like the type we frequently waylaid," she cast at him tartly, over her shoulder, "I probably would have seen through your dastardly game ere it was too late. But to deliberately plot my wretchedness and heartache by trapping me into falling in love with you as Dan, then conveniently abandon the game at his execution, leaving me to suffer the intolerable grief of believing you dead. What evil mind could concoct such a thing?"

"If you have completely finished, I shall endeavour to explain!" he seized this opportunity to have his say. "Shall we go back to the beginning?"

As his explanation had every prospect of being a long one, the Marquess considered it wiser to be seated after all, and made his way over to the bed upon which he lowered himself apprehensively.

"Let me state at the outset, when I assumed the role of Black Dan," he began, an unmistakable element of regret in his voice, "I could not possibly foresee the disastrous results. I did so simply to discourage you from your reckless pursuit; but on discovering your desperation to quit my house, I deemed it a good way to assist you in your ambition without wounding your self-respect—or mine."

"Y-You mean, every coin and trinket you gave me were from your own coffers?" she gasped, appalled.

"Naturally," he responded with hauteur. "Highway robbery is not one of my favourite pastimes."

"B-But the coaches we waylaid—the valuables we took?"

"Were returned discreetly to their rightful owners."

Christina was speechless, too much so to feel humiliated.

"Don't flatter yourself by thinking 'twas done entirely for your benefit. At the time you were well aware of how much I relished your company at Barrington Hall. I reasoned, the sooner you acquired your riches the sooner you'd be off my hands, apart from which, being your guardian, I was responsible for you. When I realised you were intent on playing highwaymen, I had to play too. Had you met up with the real Dan, I doubt if you would now be alive to boast of the fact. Capering about in the dead of night on a desolate highway—and with an unprimed pistol more often than not—the very thought curdles my blood, what's left of it. Had you no fear?"

"I-I didn't stop to think," she confessed ruefully, suddenly brought face to face with her folly. "I-I'm sorry," she grudged him, sullenly. "I seem to have put you to a deal of trouble."

"That is the most thundering euphemism I have ever heard!"

"It-It seemed an excellent idea at the time," she vindicated herself.

"Obviously I had to conceal my true identity," he resumed, "and Black Dan with his disfigured countenance appeared as good a way as any. From then onwards the sequence of events just seemed to gather momentum. I swear, I did not intend the association to last, but I must confess, I grew to enjoy our little escapades . . . they were quite a novel diversion—something I had never done before. So, I began to look forward to Friday nights—the gallops, fencing bouts, and—not least of all—the pleasure of your company. You were such a refreshing change from the normal Society female, and in my guise as Black Dan you cast aside the inhibitions which invariably shrouded you in my presence at Barrington Hall, favouring me with a glimpse of the real Christina Wansford."

Lord Stryde paused, wincing as he established himself more comfortably on the bed.

"I was quite content with this arrangement until—" he broke off with a gesture of defeat—"until it happened— what I never dreamed possible—you fell in love with the rogue." He turned to the ale beside him and poured some into the tin mug. "What could I do but try my utmost to turn you against him? And you must admit, I thrust a vast amount of effort into it—surely I deserve credit for that alone?—even, as you rationally point out, going to the preposterous length of acquiring that hideous skin, solely to shock you into forgetting me, but alas!"—his eyes flickered dubiously in her direction, wondering how she would see fit to interpret his next statement—"it was at this same time I discovered that I too, was contaminated with the disease."

"Y-You?" she gasped in disbelief, wholly betraying her outward impression of disinterest, for, despite her grim determination at the outset not to hearken to a single word, she now stood enthralled, hanging upon his lips.

"Yes—I!" he flashed back with biting sarcasm. "The Marquess of Stryde— the strange being who knoweth not the meaning of the word—was in love!"

Having fired these words with painful precision and settled his outstanding score, he continued.

"I confess the knowledge threw me into something of a dilemma. I should have disclosed all there and then, as promised, but for the real Dan complicating the issue by getting hauled off to Newgate, a situation, even so, which could have been avoided had not you given licence to your rabid curiosity."

Christina hung her head contritely, consumed with remorse at the galling recollection and tone of censure in his voice, seeing herself in perspective for the first time, a picture she did not like.

"I-I'm deeply sorry, Lord Stryde," she faltered for the second time. "I-It was unforgivable of me."

The Marquess took a lingering sip of the ale in his hand, eyeing her suspiciously, uncertain of this submissiveness.

"Pride forbids me to describe in detail the agony of torment I endured. I could not, in all honesty, blame myself. Try how I may, I could see myself only as an unfortunate victim of circumstance. No doubt you recall the question I put to you in the study, and your misinterpretation of it—simply because you stubbornly refused to regard me as anything other than your sworn enemy—right down to the ring which your blind prejudice could interpret as none other's but mine. You thought I hated you, Christina!" He cursed under his breath. "It is still utterly beyond my comprehension how you could accuse me of hatred when your eyes flashed venom into my blood at every glance. You now understand why I had to ask the question at the awkward moment—to discover whether your hatred of me was personal, or merely because you saw me as a threat to your beloved Dan and your future happiness. I need not state that you left me in little doubt about your feeling for me as Marquess. So, I then had to find out if your love for Dan could possibly outweigh your intense hatred of me when I eventually revealed my identity. By the death! you convinced me beyond any shadow of doubt that nought in the wide world would ever banish your aversion to the Wicked Stryde—with the result that I somehow had to drive it into your head at the end of our harrowing confrontation, that you would never see your Dan again, that he was truly dead and gone. At the same time, notice of the real Dan's execution was announced in the most recent issue of the *Gazette* which would have amply corroborated my statement. I swear on oath, child," he vowed in earnest, "this was done purely as a last resort when all else failed, to help you overcome and forget your wretched experience, and select someone more worthy of you."

"And what made you think I should have considered anyone else?" she asked in subdued tone.

"What option had you? I realised only too well how disillusioned you would feel when the truth was known, and so, endeavoured to soften the blow." He drained the mug with a grimace and replaced it on the chair. "Unfortunately, events did not turn out as originally planned."

Christina's mind was in chaos. Questions were crowding her brain on all sides, but the one which eventually superseded all others was that concerning his father's demise.

"Apart from the threat to the man I loved," she queried calmly, at length, "would not you consider it a natural reaction for me to develop hatred for one who had, only a short while earlier, openly confessed himself to be his father's murderer?"

It was Lord Stryde's turn to look astonished. "And when, if I may make so bold, did I ever make such a confession?"

"When have you denied the responsibility of your father's death?'" she challenged swiftly.

"That, I grant you," he allowed with a shrug. "But at the same time, I have never proclaimed myself murderer. It is an established fact that he passed on naturally through a seizure."

A look of confusion transformed her face. "Why then, hold yourself to blame, my lord?"

The question seemed to pain him acutely, and Christina immediately regretted asking it.

"B-Because I caused him extreme anxiety," he replied anon, as if the words were being wrung out of him. "I-I was a bitter disappointment to him . . . a-and stood for everything he abhorred—which could only aggravate his condition. He died without granting me the forgive . . . ness . . . I . . . craved."

For the first time Christina saw him as human, an ordinary fellow-mortal racked over the suffering he had caused the father he had loved—who had died unforgiving—and she longed to offer words of consolation but everything seemed too inadequate.

"We were utter strangers," he declared with irony. "Would you believe? I was more intimate with Uncle Leonard than my own sire!"

"A-And your m-mother?" she bravely ventured, not wishing to obtrude upon his privacy.

"My mother!" he laughed derisively. "Vowed undying love for my father, bore him the heir he desired—then vanished."

"Oh, how dreadful!" exclaimed Christina so consumed with feeling that she became a little careless in her choice of phrase, and somewhat indiscreet. "How could a woman so betray the trust of the man she truly loved?"

Lord Stryde's dark eyes rose slowly to fix their sinister regard significantly upon her.

"A strange question indeed for one who stands recently condemned of the same crime—but then, is not one female very like another?"

The blood rushed to her cheeks and she quickly put her hands over her face, unable to endure the reproach in his black smouldering gaze.

"D-Do you r-regret . . . l-loving m-me?" she felt a sudden compulsion to ask, wondering why it should bother her whether he did or not.

A lengthy pause ensued which, for some unaccountable reason, she found intolerable to bear, before he confessed with an air of defeat.

"Yes . . . in all honesty, I'm afraid I do."

Christina clung to the bedpost, biting her lip to quell her turbulent emotions, which he did not seem to notice.

"I don't know what plans you entertain for the future," he resumed at length, "but it may not be as hopeless as you fear—at least, you now command sufficient wealth to tempt noblemen of highest rank, and the most fastidious of lovers—your original ambition, was it not?"

Christina, aware that she was unable to deny the truth of it, yet found the reminder painful. Somehow, it no longer mattered if she were rich or poor, if she lived the rest of her days in a palace or prison, or is she lived at all. Why, why—a tiny voice protested inside her—if she truly hated this man, had his words the power to pierce her like swords?

"I shall have no need of such wealth," she heard herself reply in an alien voice, "in a convent."

His thick black brows drew together in disapproval.

"Where you intend to incarcerate yourself for the rest of your days, I presume?"

She nodded, haltingly, face averted.

"Why, Christina? Why?" he suddenly burst out in torment, "—when I have wealth enough and position to acquire anything you want—even any *man* you want?"

"There is nothing I want," she returned, obdurately. "And certainly no man." 'Except you!' cried the voice within—to her astonishment, but which pride compelled her to ignore.

"As you wish," he sighed, at last rising from the bed, gazing wistfully round the cottage as if committing it to memory.

Instinctively, Christina stood up too—though her legs were loth to support her.

"Y-You are l-leaving?" she queried superfluously, all at once anxious to gain time.

He merely threw her a curious sidelong glance.

"Y-You are returning to Barrington H-Hall?"

"Where else?" he parried in mild surprise.

"Do you think you are well enough to ride, m-my lord? I-I could send for your c-coach?—or p-per . . . haps. . . ."—she trailed off in confusion, not knowing why she should be in a pother to detain him.

"Pray do not concern yourself further on my behalf. The devil, I am told, takes care of his own."

Christina was wringing her hands distractedly behind her as he again took up his hat in preparation to be gone, and set it on his head.

"S-Surely there is no vital hurry? You could stay just a day longer—you really do need more r-rest. . . ."

The Marquess eyed her with growing scepticism, mistrusting this new approach.

"I am anxious to be gone at the earliest, for my own convenience as well as yours."

In a fit of desperation she blurted out ere she could stop herself: "And who do you already have next in mind for your marriage partner?"

"What precisely do you imply by that remark?" he fired back scathingly.

"Your feverish haste to end our relationship seems to imply that you cherish affection for another!—your Spanish senora, perhaps?"

Lord Stryde's eyes blazed malignantly. "That insinuation is as false as it is fatuous! I see no point in you and me becoming chained to each other—even if you were willing—when we are so obviously unsuited. We are not even wed, and here we are, prostrate through mutual mistrust."

"Mistrust!" she echoed, outraged. "Downright hypocrisy, I should call it!"

"Correct me, should I be mistaken," he enlightened her in blistering undertone, "but did I not warn you that love alone might not be enough—that there was much about me you did not know, and might not like, and which could alter everything?"

Christina stood stricken, mouth agape, it suddenly dawning upon her that she had completely forgotten everything he had said at their final meeting—due partly to the terrible shock she had sustained. Gradually, it all came flowing back into her mind, and she recalled his exact words—that she would think him cowardly and deceitful, and might even hate him! She had been horrified and thought it preposterous, yet his prophecy had come true. And the crucial test? Would she have survived it any better if she had met him as prearranged, without his disguise? Would she have reviled and scorned him to a lesser degree?

The Marquess remained motionless by the door, silently observing her.

"It is pathetically evident that my words fell upon stony ground," he stated frigidly. "You understand, of course, that our relationship could never be the same? Even if you magnanimously forgave me, I'm afraid the execrable remarks you hurled in my face cut rather deeply. Though I may manage to forgive you, I could never forget."

His hand progressed to the door-knob whilst Christina stood forcing down the huge swelling in her throat, her nails digging into the palms of her hands.

"Once again it appears fate has dealt me a cruel blow, which I doubt if I shall survive as well as those gone before. Despite my loose living I consider it undeserved—though many might differ."

Christina was in an emotional turmoil and rattled her brain for some feasible reason to detain him further, but alas! none materialised. His hand was slowly turning the knob! Within seconds he would be gone!—'Stop him! Stop him!' cried the tiny voice in her heart. 'Faint! Supplicate at his feet—anything!'—but her head over-ruled.

"Your father will come for you in due course, until which time you may consider this cottage your own," he resumed in harsher tone. "All I ask in return is that you stay out of my life! I never want to set my sight upon you again and fervently wish I had never done so in the first place. Typical of your sex, wherever you go, you leave a trail of misery and heartache in your wake!"

She reeled with the impact of his words and would have fallen but for the bedpost. If he observed this he certainly gave no intimation of it as he opened the door, then hesitated as if something had suddenly occurred to him, whilst Christina shut her eyes tightly, tensing herself, convinced that she would lose her reason and run amok if he said another unkind word—but his manner had changed.

"I don't expect you to forgive me, Christina," he whispered hoarsely, labouring under tremendous strain, "though I did all any human being could possibly do to give you the happiness you craved. I now see that I overrated my capabilities. . . . I'm sorry for deceiving you, and moreover, for loving you, but it is the only good and wholesome experience I have ever known, and in spite of your poor opinion of me—I shall cherish it always."

With that, the door closed, and he was gone.

CHAPTER FOURTEEN

Christina's eyes remained transfixed to the closed door for what seemed an eternity as she stood stricken, refusing to believe he had actually gone.

What could she offer in her defence? Once again she had disregarded his warnings, adding to his intolerable burden of pain, both mental and physical, by inflicting further suffering on him whilst he lay seriously ill, crucifying him to the bed with her spiteful tongue.

But the mystery was at last unveiled and her eyes wide open to the intense love she bore him irrespective of the name he chose—but with the realisation was the harrowing knowledge that she must face the future alone. He had not been gone out of her life two minutes and already she found the heartache unbearable! How then, was she to survive it a lifetime? Continually desiring him, and craving for the fulfilment of his love? Never again to thrill to the touch of his lips, nor caress of his hands?

Suddenly the storm burst from her as full import of her

tragic loss coupled with the strain of the past weeks overwhelmed her, and she fell upon the couch surrendering to it utterly, relinquishing all hope for her future happiness. Her torrent of grief knew no bounds, increasing in intensity until she was seized by a madness and, just as she had lain on this same worn battered couch in a frenzy of hatred, she now lay demented with desire for him, crying aloud for him to rid her of this unbearable agony, her nails clawing chunks from the rotten upholstery in her tempestuous passion, yearning for his love as she had never yearned for anything before—until a sudden movement close by caught her attention and, glancing up—shot off the couch as if it had taken fire, to stare, trembling in awe and bewilderment, at the object of her torrid desire.

The Marquess stared back at her—almost as bewildered as she—an ominous red stain contrasting vividly with the whiteness of his torn shirt. A tense silence pervaded the atmosphere as they stood thus, until Christina could endure it no longer.

"V-Val . . . en . . . tine? . . . P-Please forgive m-me? I-I've caused y-you . . . so much s-suff . . . ering . . . Wh-Why didn't you j-just let . . . me d-die in the . . . b-barn?" she sobbed, sinking to her knees to further her supplication. "I-I'm desperately sorry—but it c-couldn't possibly be any w-worse than I've suffered! . . . I-If I had only known when I u-uttered those monstrous ac-accusations, I swear, I should have cut out my tongue rather than cause you one moment's p-pain. . . . How was I to know you were the same man who drove me insane with d-desire? . . . I-I'll try to atone in any way you say . . . I'll do anything . . . s-suffer anything . . . only please don't cut m-me off from you . . . I-I know I'm not fit to be your

M-Marchioness, b-but I'll be a—a—chambermaid, k-kitchenmaid—anything—but p-please don't . . . s-send me . . . away—"

The Marquess broke in with a groan. "For heaven's sake, Christina—get up."

She scrambled to her feet, anxious to please—but eluding his gaze.

"On no less than three occasions I have had you begging and petitioning at my feet for some confounded cause or other, which I dislike most damnably!" he protested irritably. "Before aught else, you must learn that the Marchioness of Stryde does not grovel at the feet of anyone—not even her husband."

He raised up her face to meet his intense regard which she returned with a look of blank stupefaction. In fact, it was not until his manner underwent a sudden change that she began to sense his meaning.

"Christina, my dearest life, do you understand what I'm trying to say?" he whispered ardently.

"Y-You mean—"

Her words were cut short as the Marquess, refusing to waste any more time, dragged her to him in a crushing embrace, his lips smothering hers in a kiss so demanding it would seem that nothing would ever satisfy his intense craving, impervious to the racking pain in his side as he strained her to him in an iron grip, raining kisses on her upturned face, he and she so emotionally distraught that everything outside their immediate world ceased to exist, as my lord continued to prove his overwhelming love for his former ward more effectively than all the words in the King's English.

Christina clung to him wildly, feverishly, expecting him to disappear into her frenzied imagination, not trusting herself to utter a syllable for it would not make sense and he would think she had indeed gone raving mad! Instead, she relinquished herself to ride recklessly on the crest of his passionate wave, her head reeling as his burning lips scorched her neck and shoulders, before he finally buried his face in her hair with a groan.

"Oh, Christina . . . Christina . . . you can't imagine what hell I've been through!" he gasped at length, into her avid ear. "I never thought it possible that one could suffer so much and still go on living! You have driven me demented over the past months. To have you there before mine eyes, 'neath my roof, yet be compelled to deny myself! To worship you from afar, unable to touch you, or even unburden my heart by telling you—by the saints, my self-control has never survived such a crucifying ordeal!"

Christina rested her head on his shoulder and sobbed convulsively as the rapture of the moment tore her emotions apart.

"Don't cry, dear heart," he implored her huskily. "I shall not send you away—not now, I swear on sacred oath!"

This had the tranquilling effect intended and she lay contentedly in his arms, wanting nothing more than to remain thus till the end of time with his impassioned reassurances of love ringing in her ears, knowing he wanted her as desperately as she wanted him.

And so they remained for what seemed an eon of time, murmuring their undying love each for the other amidst earnest entreaties for forgiveness on either side, until this first blaze of passion gradually diminished and Christina stole a glance up at her Marquess to reward him with a shy smile, sending his pulses racing afresh.

"I couldn't leave you. Christina, I couldn't! All the

time I was saddling Pegasus I tried to tell myself I didn't need you—didn't want you!—that you were nought but a thorn in my flesh—an undisciplined, insolent, cumbersome, meddling minx whom I was well rid of, and ought never to have accepted into my house in the first place— that you had turned my entire household upside down, and completely disrupted my well-organised way of life. But before I had even taken up the reins I realised I was convincing no one—least of all, myself. And so, I dismounted intoning a different chant! 'You're a fool, Stryde!' cried I. 'You wouldn't endure the week without her. You love her and she's going to be your wife even if she despises you for the rest of her days and damns your soul to perdition. She's yours, and by Lucifer, she's going to remain so!"

However, although a warm glow swelled within her bosom at this endorsement of his devotion and undertaking to make her his bride, Christina, it may be said, did not take very kindly to his rather derogatory choice of adjectives and abruptly raised indignant head to pierce him with outraged eye, though admittedly with an unmistakable dimple in evidence at the corner of her mouth.

"Undisciplined!" she ejaculated. "Insolent!"

"An opinion I formed when first you gave voice, dear one—and I might add, which you have since done little to transform."

"Indeed, my lord!" she exclaimed. "You yourself can hardly claim to have been any less offensive on that occasion—subjecting me to the most humiliating scrutiny I have ever had the misfortune to endure, and going on to call me an impoverished draggle-tailed termagant!"

The Marquess managed with difficulty to maintain a

sober visage. "a view I still uphold—though, mayhap, a trifle less impoverished—"

Christina choked on a sharp intake of breath.

"—which in comparison, is really quite complimentary to what you ultimately termed me."

His future wife closed her ready-open mouth and gulped hard, conscious of misgivings.

"I-It is?" she stammered dubiously, wondering which part of the stormy past he now had in mind.

"You do not recall?"

On the contrary, she could recall a good many things, all equally uncivil, but was naturally reluctant to say so.

"Correct me if I do you an injustice, but I believe your choice of adjectives was—a pigheaded, infuriating, abominable, ill-mannered monster. Am I right?"

Her face turned from ashen through several shades of pink to the deepest red.

"D-Did I say that, m-my lord?" she faltered, her wide green eyes staring up into his with angelic innocence.

"However that, I am loth to say, is not what finally took the prize."

A pained expression crossed her face. "I-It isn't?"

"My dear young lady," he informed her on a note of censure, drawing her gradually back into his arms, "surely you are aware that you bear the singular distinction of being the first person to have called Valentine Francis Louis Maximilian Barrington, fifth Marquess of Stryde, a trumped-up, coarse-grained, gutter-brat—and lived to see another dawn?"

CHAPTER FIFTEEN

After completing a hasty toilette, Christina sat down to dine with her lord on humble though plentiful fare, her long chestnut-hair flowing about her shoulders, and her green eyes sparkling with an inner glow.

The first several minutes of the meal were expended in silence as she alleviated her hunger with a generous portion of veal pie, and the Marquess sampled the barley bread, deeming it something of a novelty—if little else.

"Am I permitted to ask how you came by your distinctive—er—viands?" he queried, regarding bread and cheese askance. "I am loth to think you appropriated them from my kitchens—anticipating the need, perchance, *en route* to London."

Christian returned a look of apprehension. "I-I bought them from Melstead's Farm over yonder, my lord. I'm sorry if they aren't up to your customary standard, but Dame Melstead assured me that they were quite freshly made and—"

"You sound on exceeding good terms with this Dame Bedstead?"

"Melstead," giggled Christina. "You must know the Melsteads, my lord? They are, after all, your own tenants."

"I assure you, my love, that I do not expend the night reciting parrot-fashion the names of the three hundred-odd farmers on my estates," he enlightened her genially, engrossed in the unique experience of removing the firmly adhered shell from a boiled egg. "And the farmer's good dame suspected nought amiss?"

"No, my lor—"

"Valentine," he prompted.

"Er—V-Valentine," she dutifully amended.

"Nor the good farmer?" he pressed, mildly curious.

Christina shook her head. "At least, no one was interested in me, but the labourers greatly admired Pegasus."

"Ah!" was all he commented, but with a deal of meaning. Then added cheerfully to raise her crestfallen visage: "There is no need to feel affronted, my dear. Though you may not appreciate it, you were vying with excellent pedigree stock—which simply means that I must lose no time in forwarding notification of our forthcoming marriage to the *Gazette* before your reputation is painted as black as mine."

Christina gaped at him incredulously, pie poised on wooden spoon. "Because of a mere horse?"

The Marquess spluttered, coughed, and had urgent recourse to his cider.

"A mere horse!" he echoed, appalled. "I'll have you know, my girl, that the noble animal you so contemptuously designate, set me back to the tune of some six

214

hundred guineas—and was sired by a great-grandson of the Byerly Turk!"

His future wife, however, was in no wise impressed.

"Pooh! How naïve of me to believe your concern on the night of my arrival to be on my behalf, when you warned me not to ride him," she remarked with mock coyness.

A whimsical smile lurked round the Marquess's lips. "Alas! my own, night-black stallions of Turkish extraction are something of a rarity, more so, I might add, than shapely wenches, no matter how beautiful."

"Y-You mean that the farmer will know who the horse belongs to?" she breathed in concern. "A-And the farmer's wife will know—"

"In which case by now, dear child, everyone in the entire county of Hampshire will know."

"E-Everyone? M-My father?"

But the Marquess was inexplicably interested in the damp dingy ceiling of a sudden.

"Your—er—father has known of the possibility of our"—cough—"marriage since he left prison." As his affianced seemed disinclined—or unable—to speak he went on in deepest sincerity. "I gave you my word, Christina—though you have reason to doubt it—that I did not barter your life for that of your father in securing his release. At the time it was arranged I had no intention of marrying you whatsoever. The only ulterior motive I had—as I told you—was to get you out of my house and back to your native Yorkshire. It was not until I paused to give due consideration to what my life would be with you gone out of it that I began to cherish qualms . . . and suffered a complete change of heart, so besought your father to let me care for you on a permanent basis—should

215

you prove willing—little realising what lay in store between us in the study, or that the pair of us would bid fair to quitting the world soon after!"

Christina reached across the bowl of baked apples to place a penitent hand on his arm, her beautiful eyes consumed with remorse.

"I-I'm dreadfully sorry f-for everything, V-Valentine. I shall bitterly reproach myself for the rest of my days for the trouble I brought you, and my foolhardiness which almost cost you your life."

"Which you saved quite admirably, did you not?" he parried gently.

She bit her lip in torment. "P-Please don't torture me further by offering me gratitude, my lord. Heaven knows, I deserve no credit for what I did."

The Marquess took her hand and raised it to his lips. "You will be made to pay for all the suffering you have caused me, my adorable one, but I somehow doubt if you'll find the reckoning unpleasant."

"How can you ever forgive me for dragging you into such a mess?"

"I fail to see where I was dragged?" countered his lordship, eyebrows raise. "On the contrary, I barged in of my own volition with my eyes wide open. The error I made was in turning my back on Cousin Charles. I ought to have known better! And whereas I shouldn't dream of offering you my gratitude for what you did, Christina," he whispered softly, stroking her cheek with an affectionate forefinger, "I vow on solemn oath, you have earned my undying admiration."

She flushed with pride, deeply conscious of his adoring gaze.

"What I find difficult to understand, Valentine, is how

your cousin could have known so much about me—more than I knew myself!"

"Alas! Good judgement of character cannot be said to number 'mongst your many talents, my love, for not only were you ready to place your implicit faith in my cousin—but his helpmate, Mistress Anders."

"M-Molly? Molly A-Anders was his accomplice?"

" 'Twas she, I believe, led you to Withey Hill, like a lamb to the sacrificial altar, and deserted you—after placing my cousin's note, supposedly from Tony, where your sister was sure to find it—and who, furthermore, attempted to bully your sister's maid into silence when the girl wanted to confess the whole to me. Fortunately Daisy Bigsley—I think that is her name—bravely defied Miss Anders, otherwise I doubt if I should have arrived in time to save you."

"But why did you come as Dan, and not as yourself?"

The Marquess frowned down at the offending cheese. "If I had, would you have trusted me as readily as you did your highwayman?" he challenged her, a hint of sadness in his voice. "Would you have truly believed that I'd had no part in the foul deed—and that I did not mean to harm you?"

Christina's eyes wavered and fell before the accusation.

"As Molly Anders knew that I had ridden out to Withey Hill, it did not take her long to deduce who the highwayman was who rescued you—and had no sooner done so, than she was on the doorstep of Wylton Weir babbling the news into the very attentive ear of my cousin, in the wild hope of his eventually marrying her, when he came into the title, and making her his Marchioness. Faith, how foolish women can be."

"So that was why she suddenly disappeared and I was placed in the care of the orgress—"

"The *what*?" exclaimed his lordship, mug suspended.

"I-I mean, M-Mistress Proudfoot," amended Christina, abashed.

"Extremely apt, I must confess," chuckled her future spouse. "She should be quite flattered when I tell her—"

"Valentine! Y-You wouldn't dare!"

"Wouldn't I?" he parried, quizzing her. "Surely that cannot be fear I detect in your voice, my angel—and of my former governess?"

"W-Was she, Val-Valentine?" she breathed in awe, apparently deeming him braver for having endured this fate than the one meted out by his cousin. "How on earth did you survive such rigid discipline?"

His chuckle gave way to a hearty laugh. "At least she is completely trustworthy, whereas your Molly Anders . . ."

"Yes, fancy! Molly of all people! Whoever would have thought it!" Her mind wandered on, momentarily distracted from her baked apple. "I wonder where she is?"

"Dead," obliged the Marquess bluntly.

"D-Dead? M-Molly—dead?"

"Her body was discovered the following morn in the woods—not the reward she was expecting, I'll warrant."

"Poor Molly!" lamented Christina, spirits downcast—which the Marquess refused to allow.

"Why, pray?" he queried with scorn, esteeming the bread he was lavishing gooseberry preserve upon of more concern than the worthless existence of a double-dealing servant. "She was ready to sacrifice the life of her mistress merely to further her own selfish interests. Besides which, knowing Charles so intimately, she must have been well aware of the danger she was courting."

"And to think I trusted her so. . . . I haven't been very circumspect, have I, my lord?"

"No, my love," concurred his lordship with a reproving eye.

Silence again descended—Christina biting her lip, flashing sheepish glances across the table, whilst Lord Stryde replenished his mug for the second time, nurturing a faint suspicion that he was about to be rendered yet another apology and acknowledging it a certainty when she turned a look of the most abject contrition full upon him.

"V-Valentine," she ventured in a whisper, as if taking a sacred vow, "I promise faithfully never to defy you again, no matter how strong the provocation—an-and I shall try very hard to be a good dutiful wife."

The Marquess drained his mug and thudded it down on to the table—which would have proved fatal to his delicate crystal at Barrington Hall.

"You will do no such thing, Christina! I absolutely forbid it!" he repudiated emphatically. "You will remain exactly as you are!"

His future Marchioness regarded him in amazement. "I-I will, m-my lord?"

"Wilting submissive females bore me to distraction! I prefer my women—er—woman to have spirit, to be a challenge—which is what attracted me to you in the first instance."

"So that you may administer the same punishment you did then—when I first trespassed on your highway?" she smiled mischievously.

The Marquess laughed. "That, I imagine, will be a frequent occurrence at Barrington Hall in future—if the past year is aught to go by," he responded, rising from the table and guiding her over to a chair by the fire. "However, if I were to belabour you from now till the crack of doom I doubt if it would recompense the provocation I withstood at the ball, at your persistence in favouring the all-too-eager attentions of my cousin. Had it not jeopardised the entire evening for Becky and Tony I should have had you over my knee there and then before all and sundry, and damned the consequences!"

Christina felt obliged to agree as she settled herself at his feet before the blaze, her head resting on his knee—content to sit thus amusedly watching the coloured flames dancing up the chimney, while the Marquess contemplated her delightful profile.

"Valentine," she anon ventured curiously, "if you did not wish me to favour your cousin's attentions why didn't you have him removed—by force?"

The Marquess looked a trifle shamefaced. "Because I had—er—baited my trap with great precision into which he was progressing deeper every second—and I almost had him snared when—"

"I was the bait?" she cried aghast, bobbing up from his knee.

"I assure you, it was not part of my plan that he should get so near to devouring you, my love, and he certainly would not have done so had not you treated poor Tony so shockingly—"

A peculiar squawk erupted from Christina.

"M-Mr. W-Wilde . . ." she gasped, the epitome of guilt, "i-in the s-summer . . . house! I-I quite f-forgot. S-Someone found him?"

The Marquess raised his eyes—where lurked a distinct twinkle belying his grave countenance.

"Yes, he was found," he returned without a trace of

humour, though the twinkle persisted. "His indignant cries were first heard by your sister, so I believe."

"W-Was he very angry, Valentine?" she dared to ask.

"Angry? No, dear one," he replied, tongue-in-cheek. "He wasn't angry."

"H-He wasn't?"

"No, I shouldn't term it anger, exactly—er—perhaps more in the nature of a fit—"

"A fit!"

"—of apoplexy," he rounded off casually.

"What!"

"Purely in concern for your safety, you understand, 'tis not his style to bear a personal grudge, which is one of his most endearing qualities." He heaved a sigh of forlorn hope. "Alas, if one could only say likewise of his doting betrothed."

"B-Becky?" breathed the stricken Christina.

"I hesitate to state, my own, that she was not very amused at your treatment of her beloved Tony. You—er—appreciate, you have completely shattered his faith in the fair sex?"

"Oh, Valentine," she besought him in desperate appeal, gazing up into his pale handsome face—paler than usual due to the suffering he had borne. "D-Do you think she will understand?—that she will ever forgive me?"

The Marquess cast aside his banter and drew her up on to his knee to enfold her in his arms—unable to endure any longer the anguish in those beautiful eyes.

"Christina, by the time you arrive back at Barrington Hall she'll be so relieved to see you actually alive that she'll be prepared to forgive you anything!—likewise, your father."

"Y-You truly think so?" she probed hopefully.

"I give you my word."

"As you gave it once before?" she reminded him, favouring him with a demure smile. "To find me a husband?"

"And which I fulfilled, did I not?" he countered with a downward triumphant glance. "Though, as I live and breathe, I certainly did not envisage myself in the role."

"You didn't consider yourself an eligible contender for my hand?"

"On the contrary, most ineligible."

"Because of your wicked past?" she chided gently. "Really, Valentine, why condemn yourself to a lifetime of reproach simply because the term may have once applied?"

"Others also condemn me—which even you were guilty of, dear one, until a short while ago."

"But for different, more personal, reasons."

"Because you considered me a dire threat to your highwayman and your future," completed the Marquess, toying with a lock of her hair which temptingly caressed her neck. "However—you, my darling, were in no position to condemn anyone, for reasons personal or otherwise. If information concerning your own devious past ever leaked out, your reputation would be damned more assuredly than even mine."

"Then it would appear we are ideally suited, are we not, my lord?" she challenged tantalisingly, snuggling into his shoulder. "Of course, on the other hand you must agree, my recklessness proved an advantage?"

"It did?"

"Had I not ridden out on to the highway I should

never have met nor fallen in love with rascally Black Dan."

"You deem *that* an advantage?" he queried cynically. "When you might have ended up marrying, for example, the Earl of Blakewell?—that paragon of virtue who has striven throughout his three years and thirty to preserve his noble body from corruption, and which to this very day—so 'tis rumoured—remains inviolate, untouched by feminine hand?"

But contrary to being impressed, Christina wrinkled up her nose, causing his eyebrows to rise.

"I could think of nothing more repugnant than passing the night in a marriage-bed with a man so woefully inexperienced."

The Marquess was visibly shocked!—or appeared to be.

" 'Pon rep! My dear child, 'tis not at all the thing for the delicate minds of gently reared young ladies to entertain such immodest thoughts, but to consider the merits of the match from a civilised angle—er—how much can be extorted from the poor fellow for a dazzling Society wedding that will turn the whole o' London green with envy! The thrill of a lifetime! Something ne'er-to-be-forgotten!"

Still the future Marchioness of Stryde remained utterly unmoved, her mind determined to dwell upon quite another aspect.

"Our wedding doesn't have to be a never-to-be-forgotten thrill of a lifetime, Valentine," she murmured in his ear, lowering her lashes coyly and playing havoc with his heart, "—only our wedding night."

A wicked gleam flared in the Marquess's black eyes.

"Love of my life," he whispered back, preserving the magical aura as he brought his lips once more tenderly to

223

bear on hers, "you may look forward to that with confidence—once again, I pledge you my word...."

* * *

Meanwhile, the heart-rending tale of Charles Barrington's sad and sudden demise had travelled far and wide—to London itself, where it was rumoured he had been brutally done to death by highway robbers, within a few miles of his own door, to boot.

But the Polite World heaved a sigh of relief and turned on its axis to sleep easy at the news (though none would presume to admit so) whilst the tragic tale travelled from boudoir to coffee-house and bagnio, becoming sadly distorted in the process, finally relating that the dashing Mr. Barrington had been cut down in his prime by the infamous Black Dan, scourge of the Hampshire Highways—this seeming to strike no one as at all strange, particularly as Black Dan himself, at whose door the blame was being laid without any qualms, had already bid farewell to the world via Tyburn Gallows, some weeks previous.